Get Your
Coventry Romances
Home Subscription NOW

And Get These
4 Best-Selling Novels
FREE:

LACEY
by Claudette Williams

THE ROMANTIC WIDOW
by Mollie Chappell

HELENE
by Leonora Blythe

THE HEARTBREAK TRIANGLE
by Nora Hampton

A Home Subscription! It's the easiest and most convenient way to get every one of the exciting Coventry Romance Novels! . . .And you get 4 of them FREE!

You pay nothing extra for this convenience: there are no additional charges. . .you don't even pay for postage! Fill out and send us the handy coupon now, and we'll send you 4 exciting Coventry Romance novels absolutely FREE!

SEND NO MONEY, GET THESE
FOUR BOOKS
FREE!

━━━━━━━━━━━━━━━━━━━━━━━━━━━

C0182

MAIL THIS COUPON TODAY TO:
COVENTRY HOME
SUBSCRIPTION SERVICE
6 COMMERCIAL STREET
HICKSVILLE, NEW YORK 11801

YES, please start a Coventry Romance Home Subscription in my name, and send me FREE and without obligation to buy, my 4 Coventry Romances. If you do not hear from me after I have examined my 4 FREE books, please send me the 6 new Coventry Romances each month as soon as they come off the presses. I understand that I will be billed only $9.00 for all 6 books. There are no shipping and handling nor any other hidden charges. There is no minimum number of monthly purchases that I have to make. In fact, I can cancel my subscription at any time. The first 4 FREE books are mine to keep as a gift, even if I do not buy any additional books.

For added convenience, your monthly subscription may be charged automatically to your credit card.

☐ Master Charge   ☐ Visa
42101   **42101**

Credit Card #_____

Expiration Date_____

Name_____
(Please Print)
Address_____

City _____ State _____ Zip _____

Signature_____

☐ Bill Me Direct Each Month **40105**
Publisher reserves the right to substitute alternate FREE books. Sales tax collected where required by law. Offer valid for new members only. Allow 3-4 weeks for delivery. Prices subject to change without notice.

A Season
For The Heart

by

Elizabeth Chater

FAWCETT COVENTRY ● NEW YORK

For M.T.C.
A Man after my own heart

A SEASON FOR THE HEART

Published by Fawcett Coventry Books, CBS Educational
and Professional Publishing, a division of CBS Inc.

ISBN: 0-449-50238-4

Printed in the United States of America

First Fawcett Coventry printing: January 1982

10 9 8 7 6 5 4 3 2 1

One

MISS MELPOMENE RAND staggered the last hundred yards down the highroad toward the Climbing Man Inn. She was almost blinded by the driving rain, and she was drenched to the skin. Although it was barely noon, lights gleamed from all the windows through the gray haze of the storm. Clenching her fists for a last effort, Pommy admitted to herself that she could not have gone much farther. Visions of herself lying in a ditch, all—or perhaps only partly—covered by icy rainwater, flitted through her mind. In the novel she had been reading by candlelight in her room for the last few evenings, the Heroine, one Indefensa, had been left for dead in just such a storm-battered ditch by *bandidos* who had stopped her coach and robbed her of all her jewels and money. Although her own situation was nothing like that of the girl in the novel, Pommy, recalling Indefensa's sad plight, shivered and hastened toward the warmth and safety of the inn.

The loneliness of the life she had lived since her grandfather died had forced the girl into her greatest, in fact her only, comfort—reading. Her uncle's library was a shabby holding, nothing like the wonderful, if predominantly scholarly, collection her grandfather had shared so happily with her, but Pommy had been able to borrow a number of Romances from the daughters of her mother's old friends, and even once in a while from Mrs. Appledore at the inn, when travelers left them in their rooms after spending the night at the Climbing Man.

Indefensa, or, the Blighted Heroine had been the latest of these windfalls, and, to Pommy's unsophisticated mind, by far the most exciting. The dreadful experiences which befell the hapless but beautiful heroine exerted a powerful fascination upon the imagination of a girl who had never known anything but a quiet village and the home of a scholarly country vicar. Indefensa had suffered a shipwreck, from which she had been rescued at the last gasp by a gallant, if mysterious, stranger; a duel *à outrance* with herself as the prize; a kidnapping; two robberies; incarcerations both accidental and deliberate in ruined castles and city cellars. And her disappointments in Love . . . ! Poor Indefensa had been obliged to watch not one but four handsome suitors wrenched from her grasp by, in turn, drowning, a sword fight, the Black Plague and a voluptuous Rival. It seemed to Pommy, whose greatest recent miseries had been the bad temper of her aunt and the petty malice of her two cousins, that such dramatic woes as the Defenseless One suffered were much to be preferred to her own dull and uncomfortable existence.

At this moment she was jarred out of her musings by

6

tripping over the lowest of the steps leading up to the inn doorway. She was thankful for the bad weather which kept folk within doors and unable to see her clumsiness. Pommy hurried around to the rear of the inn to the kitchens, being unwilling to go through the main rooms in her bedraggled condition. Everyone who lived in Sayre Village had known the Reverend Augustus Mayo's granddaughter from a child, and she knew it would distress most of them to see to what depths Miss Melpomene Rand had fallen.

In the warm, bright, good-smelling kitchen, Mrs. Appledore exclaimed when she caught sight of Pommy. She drew the girl to the huge stove and pulled up a stool for her.

"Sit down, my dearie! You're shivering! Doll will bring you a warm drink. Whatever can you have been thinking of, then, to venture out on a day like this?"

Pommy smiled gratefully up into the plump, rosy face bent over hers. "I had to meet the mail coach. You remember that we leave for London tomorrow, and Ceci's new cloak is to be delivered here today." She smiled. "You know she could not leave without it!"

"Plymouth coach is an hour late already," sniffed Mrs. Appledore, hiding her distress at the cold, pinched look on the girl's face. "Why did they send you? And you walked, of course."

"Can you see Uncle Charles ordering his new carriage out in this weather? Besides, the grooms are busy working on it, preparing it for the trip."

"Well, you'll stay here in the warm, and dry out until the coach does arrive, Miss Pommy. If you'll excuse me now, I'll just give Doll a hand. The inns's full, what with this weather, and everyone's hungry."

After a few minutes Pommy realized that she was in the way of the bustling activity around the stove, and

7

quietly took her warm drink into the passage which led from kitchen to taproom, thinking to stand there out of the way until she had finished the hot sweet tea. But the side door from the house to the stable opened into this hallway, and it was bitterly cold. So Pommy went toward the taproom, where several high-backed settles gave privacy and protection from drafts to the tables between them. The taproom was cozy, crowded, and poorly lit. Pommy slipped unobtrusively into the first cubby, empty because it was the darkest and the farthest from the bar, and prepared to rest in the warmth until the mail coach arrived.

Exhausted by her battle with the storm, she leaned her head against the high back of the settle and drew a long, shuddering breath. She had not been seated above two minutes when she heard a gruff voice from the other side of the wooden partition. At first she could not distinguish the words above the muted clamor of voices in the taproom, but suddenly one phrase caught her attention and she turned her head to press her ear against the thin wood.

"—the Rand kerridge . . . can't miss it . . . painted red wi' yella wheels . . . women's sparklers . . . store of cash—"

Pommy stiffened. The Rand carriage! A second voice was murmuring.

"How many inside?"

"Squire, his missus, three girls. An abigail, too, most like."

". . . a crowd. Won't Squire ride alongside?"

"In this rain?" scoffed the gruffer voice. "If anyone goes outside it'll be the maid, or the poor relation."

"A gal? 'E'd never—"

"From all I 'ear tell, they'd as soon have her pullin' the kerridge as ridin' in it. Squire's family uses the gal

8

as a drudge ... 'er pay is as like to be a blow as tuppence."

The voices were louder now, and less guarded.

"Well, that's all of 'em inside the kerridge, then. Does Squire carry a pair o' pops?"

"—you not to worry? We'll 'ave ours out an' ready while the old gager's still figgerin' out what's to do!" The voice lowered conspiratorially and Pommy pressed her ear painfully against the wooden seat back. ". .. 'old my pops on 'em and you get the cash box. Built in under back seat, it is—about the middle—"

The other voice rose in a sharp whine. "Let *me* 'old 'em up, an' you get the dibs an' sparklers, Quint!"

"Stow yer gab!" came the sharply hissed order. Then after a moment's silence, "Why're you so 'ot to 'andle the barkers, Jib?"

"It's not so much what I *wants* as what I *don't* want," admitted Jib in a subdued whine.

"What's that 'sposed to mean?" growled Quint.

"Don't want to be fumblin' around 'mongst all them females' skirts to find the cash. You gotta figger them women'll be screamin' an' kickin' an' carryin' on like Bedlam—"

This excuse was greeted with coarse laughter. "We can 'ave 'em all out onto road whilst you nabbles the dibs. Never figured you to be scared of a bunch of skirts!"

"It's what's in 'em," pleaded his companion. "I can't abide historical females."

"Maybe you think we should shoot 'em all first?" sneered the leader.

Pommy waited to hear no more. She turned and ran down the narrow passageway toward the kitchen, her heart pounding in her chest. So extreme was her agitation, and so dark the passageway, that she caromed headlong off a huge male figure which was just entering the inn through the stable doorway. Strong arms shot out to steady her, and she was clasped against a wet riding cloak.

"What have we here?" queried a lazy, good-humored voice.

"Oh, sir," gasped Pommy, peering up through the gloom in an effort to discern the face above her, "there are highwaymen in the taproom who are planning to rob my uncle's carriage tomorrow!"

There was a silence, during which the Stranger continued to hold Pommy's wet and shivering body comfortably close. Then he said, "And what would you do, child, if I were one of the conspirators, just coming in to join the council?"

Pommy lifted her chin. "Give me credit for some perception, sir! Your voice is that of an educated man, and your—your attire suggests that highway robbery is not necessary to support you."

The Mysterious Stranger threw back his head with a shout of laughter. "To think that I should be blessed with such an encounter at the Climbing Man! It is pure Cheltenham! Let me ask you, madame, could I not be a nobleman fallen upon hard times, who is seeking to recruit his fallen fortunes by consorting with a gang of footpads?"

"Highwaymen," corrected Pommy absently, but her heart had lifted with a thrill of delight. No one had ever entered into her fantasies so directly, so richly, before! It was unbearable that, at the moment when she seemed to have found a kindred spirit, the fantasy should be reality, and the amused sharing of the game a hindrance to saving her family from disaster.

The Stranger noted her unconscious sigh, and the steadiness with which she faced his scrutiny. "You are serious, then? What evidence can you produce, Cassandra?"

Added pleasure! The Stranger was literate, acquainted with the Greek tale of Priam's daughter, "prognosticating woe"—and invariably correct in her gloomy prophecies!

Somehow she did not feel alarm at the comfortable clasp in which the gentleman still held her. She said, in her clear soft voice, "I have just overheard two men in the next-to-last booth in the taproom discussing the robbery of Squire Rand's carriage on its way to London tomorrow. They decided they would do the job between Bodmin and Launceston. Their names are Quint and— uh—Jib."

The big man's arms tightened a little and then released her. "You *are* serious, then. There is no denying the down-to-earth validity of such names as Quint and—uh—Jib."

Although he was still teasing her, Pommy heard the note of decision in his deep voice.

"Suppose you continue to the kitchen or wherever you were heading so hastily to get help, and I shall reconnoiter the terrain. Meanwhile, say nothing to anyone."

"May I not wait for you here?" pleaded Pommy. "It is too much to hope that Mrs. Appledore would not get it out of me, if I go to the kitchen now." She said awkwardly, "She is a good woman, and has known me all my life."

"You had better come with me, then. I do not wish you to be hanging about in this drafty passage. Did you not realize you are soaked to the skin? It is not at all the thing, you know," the Stranger said sternly.

Pommy crept after his huge figure as it moved, cat quiet, toward the taproom. At her direction, they slipped into the rear cubby, still mercifully empty, and the Stranger leaned his head against the wooden settle back as Pommy had done earlier. For a long moment he waited, frowning, and was just turning away when his attention was suddenly arrested. He listened, then motioned Pommy back into the passage. Following her, he said quietly, "There is something afoot. Is your carriage in the stable—no, wet as you are, you did not come in a carriage. Did you ride or walk?"

"Walked," said Pommy.

"Then return to your home at once. Do not mention this adventure to your family. I shall recruit Appledore and the village constable to deal with these bravos." His handsome face broke into a wide grin of pleasure. "You have succeeded in brightening a day I had condemned as the most boring of my life, caught in this less than scintillating hamlet by the storm and a broken axle. My thanks, madame! No, I must know your name—if you please?"

"I am Melpomene Rand," the girl said shyly.

"Your parents surpassed themselves," complimented the Stranger. "Melpomene—one of the Muses, surely?"

"Patron of Tragedy and lyre playing," explained Pommy. "My grandfather frequently said it had influenced my imagination to Romantic excesses."

The Stranger smiled so warmly that Pommy's heart began pounding again. "Now home with you to safety, Melpomene Rand, and let your champion do battle for your family."

Pommy hesitated.

"You prefer that I should not interfere in your personal melodrama?" inquired the big gentleman, smiling. "Perhaps I should have consulted you. What was it your intention to do about this challenge, had I not come upon the stage?"

12

"I had thought," said the girl, "to save them all, and die in the attempt. That would teach them a lesson."

"Indeed? But is that not rather extreme? Why would you not rather warn them of what you overheard, so that they might either postpone their journey or take enough servants to foil the attempt? Thus earning their undying gratitude?"

Pommy appeared displeased with these alternatives. "It would not do at all. To begin with, they would say it was just another of Pommy's silly starts, and then, when it was proven true, they would say I should have warned them. It would do no good to remind them that I had done so. They would not believe me. In either case, gratitude would be the last emotion they would feel."

"Had you considered," inquired the Stranger in a rather less humorous tone, "that you might be killed in Act One, as it were, and never discover whether the other victims were impressed by your sacrifice, since they themselves might also be dead?"

Pommy considered this, and finally nodded her head reluctantly. "You are right, of course. It would have been selfish of me to expose them to danger just so that I might die and cause them remorse. In such case, also, the whole thing would be useless, since I should not be present to observe their grief, if any."

"Not quite the *whole* thing," objected the gentleman with what Pommy took to be irony. "The highwaymen at least would have cause to thank you. Perhaps if they Knew All, they might be persuaded to make you a member of the gang—*post mortem*."

This startled her into a chuckle, which the Stranger heard with relief. "I see you are funning me," Pommy said.

"On the contrary, I myself have frequently wished I

might see some of my own relatives in a pickle. I must confess I had no thought of perishing in the attempt myself, however. One would surely choose to live to hate another day?"

"I don't *hate* them," explained Pommy sadly. "And I had not considered that they might be hurt. They are none of them the sort who would put up a struggle, you see! More likely to hand over the jewel cases in a hurry, and scream with rage later. I had the notion that I might be the one injured, so that they would be sorry they had behaved as they did to—a penniless orphan."

Then seeing his faintly mocking smile, the girl continued in a low, anguished voice, "It is easily seen that you have never been cold shouldered, and mocked at, and set to do the most menial tasks, and never let to go to the parties or picnics! Much less had your appearance made fun of!"

"How do you know none of these admittedly very unpleasant things has ever happened to me?" asked the Stranger, his voice a little gentler.

"Anyone but a perfect goose could tell it after one glance at you," retorted Pommy. "You are, first of all, a man, and if anyone did attempt to treat you so, you could walk out and get a position on a ship going to America or India, and make your fortune. Or sign on as a soldier and fight with distinguished courage in foreign wars—"

"We are temporarily at peace," the man reminded her.

"Now you are laughing at me," said the Blighted Heroine.

"Yes, I am," agreed the Stranger, "and so would you, if you would give your mind—your reasoning faculty, not your imagination—to the problem for five minutes. I quite admit that a female could not follow either of the two colorful courses you named, but is it not true that there are situations open to a girl of your obvious breeding and education which might offer you some measure of satisfaction?"

"Name one," requested the girl succinctly.

The gentleman hesitated. "Governess?"

"I am too young, and have neither the formal training nor the means of getting any. My education was given to me by my grandfather, and is solely classical and literary. A governess needs to excel in pianoforte, embroidery, china painting and deportment, as well as French and history."

"Companion to an elderly lady of good family?"

"What elderly lady? Besides not knowing any such, nor having any person who would be willing to recommend me to one, I cannot believe that you yourself would be willing to dance attendance upon some ancient invalid who would, besides being cross as crabs, desire you to read sermons to her, walk her bad-tempered poodle, and spoon her gruel into her palsied mouth!"

Her companion cast her a revulsive look. "No," he admitted, "I should not enjoy anything so Gothic as the activities you describe. But must all ladies desiring a companion be such crones? Surely there must be an employer—or even another occupation—less odious?"

Pommy raised one slender eyebrow.

The Stranger frowned..

After observing his cogitations pityingly, the girl finally spoke. "There is being a serving maid in some low tavern—"

"Must it necessarily be a *low* tavern?" protested the gentleman. "Mrs. Appledore would find you work, surely? You said she was kind to you."

"And how long do you think Squire Rand would

permit his orphaned niece to wait on tables at an inn within a mile of his estate?"

When the Stranger was unable to answer this question, Pommy went on, "Of course, I might run off to London—I have nearly three pounds saved—and become a kitchenmaid in a great house, having one afternoon off a month and sleeping in the attics with mice, or in the basement with rats." She awaited his palliating comment upon this grim picture, but when he made none, she went on, "There is also the faint chance that I might be lucky enough to get a post as abigail to some young miss, and carry pots of hot water up several flights, help her dress for Balls, and wait up to help her undress and hear all about her triumphs and the fun it was—" Almost in spite of herself, the young voice shook a little.

"No," said the gentleman harshly, "that solution does not really offer much attraction."

"But we are wasting time! If we do not act quickly, the highwaymen will leave the inn and we shall have no hope of saving the day!" the girl cried.

The Stranger seemed to come to a decision. "Very well, Miss Melpomene Rand. Return home as I suggested, and have no fear. Between us, Appledore and I shall find a way to thwart the would-be Road Agents, I promise you. Go to London tomorrow. Who knows? Fate may have a brighter future in store for you than at the moment seems possible."

Casting the obtuse but well-meaning stranger a glance of pity for his naiveté, and remembering to thank him politely for his assistance, Pommy turned and walked back to the kitchen, and thence out the door with just a wave to the harassed mistress and her busy maids.

When she had gone, Derek Masterson, the Earl of

Austell, sought out his host and informed him of the conversation which had been overheard in his taproom.

"Oh, that'll be Miss Pommy, poor child! She is forever discovering a mystery! But whatever was she doing in my bar, Your Lordship?"

"She had gotten herself drenched in the storm, and your good wife gave her a cup of tea and sent her in there to dry off. It seems she was waiting for the mail coach."

"What can the squire's family be thinking of, to send her out on foot in this weather just to pick up Miss Ceci's cloak?" Appledore tutted angrily. "My wife and I had great respect for her mother; the vicar's only child, she was, that married Mr. Edwin, Squire's youngest brother. Drowned they both were, when Mr. Edwin's yacht overturned. Miss Pommy was a child at the time. Went to live with Vicar, she did, and a high old time they had, poring over his books, and him teaching her what he knew about foreign languages. A real scholar was the Reverend Mayo—!"

"*Augustus* Mayo?" the Earl pricked up his ears. "I have two very fine books he wrote."

"He's dead now, and Miss Pommy's up at Highcliff Manor with Squire Rand and his lady. They don't value her as they should—" The host hesitated, aware that he was saying too much to a stranger. "Well, she is forever reading books, and thinking what she reads is the truth. That is why she made such a tale about the talk in the taproom, depend on it!"

"I also overheard the talk, and I am not a romantical miss," the Earl advised him dryly. "The men's names, by the way, are Quint and Jib."

Appledore chuckled richly. "Those sots? Milord, around here it is only innocents like Miss Pommy Rand who do not have their measure. They are in here any night they can scrape together the cost of a bottle, drinking and spinning their totty-headed schemes. It will all be forgotten by the morning, lost in the screw of a bursting head and a queasy stomach." He shook his own head in extenuation. "Their lives are very dull, Milord. Quint is one of Dr. Mannering's grooms, and Jib is a farmhand."

"You relieve my mind," said the Earl dryly. "I had visions of seeking out the constable to protect Miss Rand's family from highwaymen."

"You'd have had far to seek and little to gain from that," Appledore advised him. "Constable Swan is a dogged foe of poachers, and quite useful at finding strayed cattle, but as a thief-taker, well—" he shrugged and grimaced.

"We might send someone to relieve Miss Melpomene's fears," mused Lord Austell.

"Better not, Milord," cautioned Appledore. "The squire and his lady are very niffy-naffy, and Miss Pommy has a hard enough time with them without us telling them this latest start of hers. They say she is a widgeon, what with her romantical ideas." He shook his head regretfully. "It's the fault of too much reading of them foreign books, Milord. Quite addled her wits, Squire says."

The Earl knew a sudden illogical rage against this beef-witted Squire Rand—obviously a mutton-headed Philistine. He was tempted to make a comment quite alien to his usual detached arrogance toward chance-met persons of little breeding and less wit, when he caught himself short with a sense of shock. It was not his practice to encourage country innkeepers, nor to interest himself in the affairs of village maidens, no matter how literate. But he could not get the picture of the child's great green eyes out of his mind. Green?

18

No, rather a glowing gray-green-gold, like the sea in a storm. He was recalled to a sense of his surroundings when Host Appledore uttered a sharp exclamation.

"You addressed me, sir?" he asked, staring at the landlord who was now holding a large bundle in his arms.

"It's poor Miss Pommy, Milord. She's gone and forgotten the cape Miss Ceci sent to Plymouth for! No mistake, they'll make the child sorry for it! Probably send her back here in the rain to fetch it."

"That they shall not," vowed the Earl grimly. "Give me the wretched thing, and send my groom to hitch up my carriage. My coachman reported the new axle installed."

He strode from the taproom in a fury—with himself, with Squire Rand and his unpleasant family, but most of all with a storm-eyed, fanciful, bedraggled little waif of a girl who had somehow managed to involve him in her ridiculous affairs.

Two

POMMY STAGGERED IN the front door of Highcliff Manor as dripping wet as though she had fallen into the ornamental pond. The butler tutted crossly as she stood on the rug taking off her ruined bonnet.

"Your shoes, Miss Pommy! They are thick with mud! We shall never get it off the carpets!"

"I'll just go up the back stairs and change in my room," Pommy began, when Forte interrupted her.

"Miss Cecilia told me to tell you to go straight to her room with the cloak as soon as you returned. You've been gone a long time, Miss Pommy." Then, catching sight of her appalled expression, he asked, "What's wrong?"

Pommy's face had gone white under the splatters of mud. "The cloak!" she groaned. "I forgot it entirely, when I heard those highwaymen planning to rob Uncle's carriage on the way to London!"

Forte shook his head repressively. "Miss Pommy, when *will* you leave off this childish story-telling? There were no highwaymen, Miss Pommy! And what Miss Ceci will say when she hears—!"

"When she hears *what?*" demanded a cold, hard little voice from the stairway. Pommy's remorseful gaze lifted to see her cousin standing on the halfway landing, posed very prettily in her new pink *robe en chemise* which flattered her rose-petal complexion. With her usual acumen concerning anything which affected herself, she said sharply, "You look a wreck! Have you dropped my new cloak in the mud, then, you blundering idiot?"

"No—that is, well—you see, I—"

"Oh, stop babbling and come to my room!" With a flounce which Forte thought very vulgar indeed, Ceci turned and ran up the staircase.

"Take the back stairs, Miss," the butler advised in a hurried undertone. "If the mistress catches you walking on the carpets with those shoes—!"

Shaking inwardly with cold and alarm, Pommy made her way up the servants' staircase and down the hall to Ceci's attractive bedroom. The door stood ominously open, and within, seated on a pink velvet upholstered chair, Ceci waited with an angry face.

"Well, where is it?" she snapped, as Pommy marched into the room as courageously as she could. It did not help the culprit to perceive her cousin Lydia ensconced in another chair, a sly smile on her fubsy face. Lydia lacked the piercing rapier attack of her sister. She contented herself with heavy-handed, pseudohumorous remarks which she served up with a smile. As now.

"Don't tell me you've dropped Ceci's new cloak in the mud, poor Pommy? Even you could not be quite so awkward, I am sure!"

21

"I—I forgot to bring it," confessed Pommy, low voiced.

"You *forgot—!*" shrieked Ceci, who saved her pretty voice and charming manners for her superiors in the social world. "But you've been gone over two hours, and you had nothing else to do but pick up the cloak!"

"The coach was late," began Pommy. "Then, since I was drenched and shivering, Mrs. Appledore let me wait by the stove in the kitchen. It was while I was waiting that I heard the plot against you—"

"What plot? Have you run mad?"

"I think Pommy is giving us one of her Romantic little stories," laughed Lydia. "You know she is always dreaming up some tale with herself as the heroine, when she should be attending to her duties. Mama has often deplored her sad want of common sense."

"There were two highwaymen," Pommy persisted doggedly. "I overheard them say they would stop our coach—your father's coach—between Bodmin and Launceston—"

But Ceci had no patience with this farrago of non-sense, and leaping from her chair she ran over to Pommy and slapped her face hard. "Stop giving me a Banbury tale! You were dallying with the servants at the Climbing Man when you should have been fetching my cloak!" She slapped Pommy again, viciously. "I know what Papa will think about this!"

"To say nothing of Mama's comments," added Lydia. "I fear you have just wrecked your chances of going to London with us, poor Pommy. Still, only think what a nice rest you will have, when not assisting Forte to put the furniture under covers or washing out the cupboards! He might even let you polish the best silver!"

Holding back her tears, Pommy felt a sharper pain in her heart than the one in her cheek. *Not go to London!* Surely not even Aunt Henga could be so

22

cruel? When she had been saving all the birthday tuppences, and the Christmas shilling, and the two pounds her mother had left her, and wearing her old clothes without complaint, so that there might be enough to buy at least one new dress when she came to London! She turned her great shadowed green eyes from one cousin to the other. "Not go—?" she whispered. "You don't—you *can't*—mean it!"

"Mama never intended you to go," said Ceci impatiently. "You would overcrowd us in the carriage."

"But your papa promised I might go, and visit the Libraries and Museums! I should be happy to maid you when you needed me—if only I were free for just a little while—mornings, before you awake. . . ."

"You haven't enough alamodality to serve as our abigail and dress our hair in the latest style—" Ceci brushed away her protest.

"I can picture you traipsing about London in that dress," laughed Lydia. "You would shame us all!"

"None of your acquaintance need ever see me," pleaded Pommy. "I should slip in and out of the house by the servants' entrance."

"That dress would shame us with the smart London servants," said Lydia. "Poor Pommy!"

"My savings!" Pommy cried desperately. "Your mama said I had saved enough to afford one presentable gown!"

"But that money will have to go toward buying Ceci a new cloak *now*, will it not?" laughed Lydia. "Of course it won't be nearly enough to pay for the cloak, but I daresay in a year or so you will have the sum—"

There was a discreet knock on the door. Ceci flounced over and pulled it open angrily. The youngest footman was standing outside. "Well, what do *you* want?" Ceci demanded.

"Beg pardon, miss, but there's a gentleman asking to see Miss Pommy. Mr. Forte has put him in the small waiting room, seeing as he doesn't know the gentleman, and wouldn't risk showing him into the drawing room."

"A *gentleman?* For Pommy?" Ceci trilled a laugh. "If he's a gentleman, he's probably come to call on me—"

"Mr. Forte asked him twice, to be sure. The gent says it's Miss Pommy as he wishes to speak to. He's got a present for her."

"This," pronounced Ceci, undecided between scorn, anger, and curiosity, "I shall have to look into!" and she sailed out of her room, pink draperies flying.

Pommy ran after her, anxious at this new development and yet eager to discover who had asked for her. Since she had left her grandfather's home, no one had ever called specifically to see her, although some of the neighbors who had known her parents and her grandfather had occasionally inquired after her health and sent kind messages. Her brain was already buzzing with possibilities: A lost and forgotten relative, who had emigrated to the Colonies and made a fortune, was now wishing to see the vicar's granddaughter; a childhood friend of her father's had just now recollected his promise to see how Edwin's child went on; or perchance the caller had brought a small overdue check for the vicar's book (a critical but alas! not a commercial success). Pommy hastened down the stairs in Ceci's wake. It did not occur to her to resent the fact that her guest had been relegated to the room set aside for tradesmen and persons not vouched for.

She arrived at the door of the waiting room in time to see a flutter of pink disappearing inside. Setting her jaw bravely, she followed.

Standing very much at his ease was a man who

24

seemed to fill every square foot of the tiny cold room. It was the Mysterious Stranger from the inn! Pommy's soft pink mouth formed a soundless "O!" of surprise.

Ceci, who had already realized that the elegantly dressed gentleman with the haughty manner was neither a servant nor a tradesman, came forward in a fair imitation of her mama's social manner. "I am Miss Cecilia Rand," she began, consequentially.

The Stranger, including her in the brief bow he made to both girls, walked past Ceci to stand in front of Pommy. He indicated a large parcel lying on the table. "You forgot this," he said with a warm smile which faded as he noted her tear-stained face with the red patch burning on one white cheek.

"It is my new cloak!" cried Ceci gaily, all girlish charm and enthusiasm. "But how *gallant* of you! I was sure Pommy had lost it, the silly little widgeon! Now you must come into the drawing room and be properly thanked!" She glanced dismissively at Pommy. "Take the cloak up to my room and hang it up carefully." She offered to place her hand on the Stranger's arm, her pretty face dimpling into a smile.

The Stranger moved away slightly and slanted a cool eyebrow in her direction. "And who are you?" he asked. "I requested to speak to Miss Melpomene Rand."

Ceci brushed that aside. "Oh, Pommy is not important! She is always daydreaming and getting things in a muddle. Mama calls her shatterbrained!" with a tinkling little laugh. "I must apologize for her—dragging you here through the storm to return my cloak when you had likely more important things to do, Mr.—?"

Her obvious angling for information brought a quick blush to Pommy's face. The Stranger's self-possession was quite unruffled.

"My name is Masterson," he informed her. "I believe

25

you owe your apologies to your cousin. I had only to make a short detour on my way to London, in the comfort of my carriage. It was she who was forced to trudge through the storm." He looked at Pommy's wet garments and muddy shoes significantly.

Ceci followed his glance and gave a little shriek. "Pommy, your shoes! Get up to your room and change! Will you *never* learn how to go on properly in a gentleman's household?"

"I have always been told," remarked Masterson with an air of detachment, "that one learns best by observation of good examples."

Ceci clapped her hands girlishly, quite misreading the implied criticism. "Oh, what a charming compliment! You are a flatterer, sir!"

Pommy was forced to choke down an involuntary laugh as she caught the derisive gleam in the Stranger's eyes.

"Now you really must come into the drawing room and accept a cup of tea for your trouble—or perhaps something a little stronger?" Ceci moved toward the door, supremely confident of her charm, and almost bumped into Pommy. "Are you still here? I thought I had told you—"

"You must permit me to make my adieux to Miss Melpomene," interrupted the Stranger quietly. "I have been informed by Host Appledore at the Climbing Man, Miss Rand, that your grandfather was the Reverend Augustus Mayo. I have read and greatly admired his work—"

"Oh, poor Parson Mayo!" interjected Ceci, not at all liking the way the man lingered to talk to Pommy. "He went prosing on forever! Don't tell me you've heard of his books in London?"

"I was fortunate enough to have been able to secure a

26

copy of his latest book, Miss Rand," continued Masterson as though there had been no interruption. "It is a work of such profound scholarship as to delight while it challenges the mind."

Pommy's face was aglow with pride. She fought to keep back tears of pleasure; there had been so pitifully few who had known how to value her beloved grandfather's work.

Ceci was frowning. "Oh, are you a *grind*, as the saying is? You do not look it, sir! Pommy is bookish too. She is always weeping over some silly Tragedy from the Greeks, or mooning over poetry and Romances! My papa says it is a sad waste of time, and Mama swears Pommy has made herself into a freak." She giggled. "Even her name is outlandish—Melpomene! Have you ever heard of anything more ridiculous?"

"Frequently," smiled the big man, so coldly that Pommy wondered that Ceci did not cringe at the contempt in his voice. "But why are you wasting the talents of this learned lady in errands to the village? Has not your papa a footman or a groom who might venture to brave the elements?"

"Of course Papa has footmen and grooms," Ceci said crossly, not at all pleased at the turn of the conversation. "They have important work to do, while Pommy is frequently idle! I do not know what she has told you," she glanced suspiciously at her cousin, "but I must warn you she is forever making up taradiddles to gammon us. Why, just now she told me a cock-and-bull story about highwaymen to excuse her carelessness in forgetting my cloak—"

"But there were highwaymen, you see," the Stranger said. "Host Appledore and I dealt with them and sent them packing. It would appear your cousin has saved your family from an extremely unpleasant encounter.

27

Now I suggest that you take your cloak and leave me to talk for a moment to your cousin, in private, if you please!"

Pommy's heart sank. If only he understood the situation! The poor man was inviting the most humiliating setdown, and she herself could not think of any way to protect him from the results of his unfortunate plain speaking. Ceci's pretty mouth was already setting into the familiar ominous curve, and her brows were drawing together. She opened her mouth to deliver one of her devastating tirades. . . .

But the Stranger was not even looking at her. "What has happened to your cheek?" he asked Pommy sternly. "It looks very much as though some insensitive brute had struck you."

Ceci closed her mouth with a snap. "I shall bring Mama here to deal with you as you deserve!" she shrilled, and ran out into the hall.

With one smooth dark eyebrow lifted, the man walked over to close the door firmly. "What a virago!" he commented. "Now, Miss Rand, perhaps you will tell me what happened to your face?" Seeing her stand silent, he continued, "Did that charming little monster slap you? As a reward for your journey through the storm to fetch her garment?" He took her chin in strong, gentle fingers and turned her face up for a searching scrutiny. "No, don't pull away! Let me see your cheek!"

"I thank you, sir, for bringing her cloak," Pommy managed, keeping her eyelids down so that he might not read what was in her eyes, "but I beg you to go at once, before Ceci brings back her Mama. *She* will rail at you so dreadfully there will be no enduring it! And after you have been so kind as to deliver the cloak which I stupidly forgot!"

Without heeding her anxious remarks, the big man

led Pommy to the most comfortable of the chairs and seated her carefully. "You need a glass of sherry to warm you, then a change into dry clothing, and someone to bathe your cheek with glycerin and rosewater." He gave a sigh of exasperation. "Does no one care what happens to you, infant?"

"My aunt and uncle have been more than generous in accepting the responsibility of such a shatterbrain as myself," the girl said gloomily. "I am a constant irritation to them all."

"Then perhaps you should remove the source of the irritation?" The man called Masterson smiled at her wistful little face. "Now I have a suggestion to make. My sister-in-law is an invalid—a very beautiful and fashionable invalid, I must warn you, and not the palsied crone of your imaginings! She swears she needs a companion, but cannot abide the heavy-handed, middle-aged females she has interviewed. She told me precisely what she must have, and I flatter myself I have found it!"

"What—what does she require?" stammered Pommy, fascinated and warmed by Mr. Masterson's delightful smile.

"She wants a quiet young girl with gentle hands and voice and a compassionate nature; a young woman who is bright and intelligent, with a pleasant manner—" His handsome features took on a coaxing smile. "What do you say, Melpomene Rand?"

Melpomene stared unhappily back at him. It was of all things what she would love to do, for the idea of tending a youthful invalid—probably ethereally lovely, and hiding an aching heart bravely, or, alternately, facing a fatal illness with superb courage—thrilled her Romantic heart. Still, she must be honest with this kind and generous man.

"I am more like to drive her to an early grave," she confessed. "I forget things, fall over things, drop things! Somehow I seem to invest the simplest actions with unexpected and unfortunate consequences."

"Bravo!" smiled Mr. Masterson. "Exactly what Aurora Masterson needs! She is bored to distraction."

"My aunt will tell you that I am hopeless—stupid, blundering, a constant annoyance to persons of sensibility—"

"I think," interrupted the gentleman, "that you are very unhappy here, are you not?"

Before Pommy could answer, the door crashed open and Mrs. Henga Rand swept into the room like a ship under full canvas. Her bony nose was thrust forward, and her rather small eyes glared with outrage.

"What is this—this person doing in my house, Melpomene?" she demanded.

The Stranger made her a bow which opened her eyes.

"Allow me to present myself, madame. I am Austell."

"Austell?" Mrs. Rand looked as though she were smelling something unpleasant. "You told my daughter your name was Masterson. Are you now claiming to be in some manner related to the Earl—?"

"I am Derek Benedict Philip Masterson, Earl of Austell, Viscount Tory, Lord Amberly, etc., etc." The Earl further identified himself in a bored voice.

"You mean *you*—oh, I do not at all credit it! This is some ridiculous ploy of Pommy's—"

"I assure you, madame," said the Earl in a voice which barely disguised his contempt, "Miss Melpomene had absolutely nothing to do with my becoming the Earl of Austell."

"Austell . . . !" the angry woman spat the name, unwilling to accept the fact that she had presented a very poor appearance before a member of the Peerage.

30

She began to lash herself into one of her dreaded furies, rages she had found useful in controlling her household.

The Earl took the wind out of her sails. "It will be proper for you to address me as My Lord, or Lord Austell," he instructed her in a tone of calm condescension which Mrs. Rand found to be unbearable. Her daughter, also, it appeared, for Ceci now revealed herself from her listening post beyond the open door.

"Don't let him gull you, Mama! This is some rig he is running to gain entrance to the house!"

"I thought it was Miss Melpomene who was supposed to have a lurid imagination?" queried the Earl. "At least I have not heard her characterized as vulgar."

Mrs. Rand gasped, and *faute de mieux*, turned to wreak her vengeance upon Pommy as the prime cause of her discomfiture. "Go to your room, miss! Your uncle shall hear of this, I promise you! It will of course be impossible for you to accompany us to London after *this*! Indeed I think I shall arrange for you to go into service somewhere in this area, for I am sure I cannot be expected to provide any longer for a young woman so lost to all sense of propriety—"

"That will not be necessary," stated the Earl blandly. "Miss Melpomene has accepted a position in my sister's household."

Mrs. Rand retorted with a sneer, "I am sure *you* would find a use for her, *Your Lordship*—if you really are Austell, which I take leave to doubt! A penniless orphan, even though she was a clergyman's grand-daughter, should prove fair game to such a gentleman as yourself!"

Pommy was staring from one to another of the disputants with a wide, horrified gaze. "Aunt Henga, you cannot mean—! I have done nothing except forget

31

Ceci's cloak! I am deeply sorry to have caused her discomfort—"

"Stop crawling and show a little pluck, young Pommy," advised the Earl quietly.

"If you leave this house with this *Man*," threatened her aunt, "you will never be permitted to cross the threshold again!"

Pommy looked from the congested, furious visage of her aunt to the imperturbable countenance of Lord Austell. She straightened her slender shoulders and lifted her head. "Very well, Aunt Henga. I shall pack my things at once. Since I am to be your sister's companion My Lord, may I have her address in London?"

A sneer twisted Mrs. Rand's lips. "His sister's companion, is it? Well, that's one name for it! Pack your things and get out! I shall send Forte up with you to make sure you do not take anything which does not belong to you."

"I shall await you outside in my coach, Miss Rand," the Earl advised her. "With your permission, I shall escort you to Lady Masterson. The journey to London might prove difficult for you, alone."

Mrs. Rand left the room with a flounce reminiscent of her daughter's, seizing the stunned Ceci by the arm as she passed her. The two left in the room heard her loud voice as she instructed the butler that the parson's brat was leaving them for a Life of Sin, and demanding that Forte send someone up to her room to see that she took nothing but what was her own.

Regarding the girl's shocked face intently, the Earl said, "I think even the life which your aunt mistakenly envisions for you would be better than what you have had to endure in this house, if this is a fair sample of it."

Pommy bowed her head briefly, unwilling to make a

32

comment. Then she forced her wide green eyes to meet his. "I shall not keep you waiting, Milord. There is not much to pack. But it seems an imposition that you should have to carry me to London in your own carriage."

"Pack, child," advised the Earl briefly.

He accompanied her into the hall, which was now empty save for the shocked Forte and one of the maidservants.

"Miss Pommy!" the butler moaned. "What is to become of you?"

The Earl, giving Pommy a gentle push toward the waiting maid, turned his attention to Forte. "I am Austell. Miss Rand will be quite safe in Portman Square under Lady Masterson's aegis," he said quietly. "My sister-in-law is an invalid, in need of a gentle and sprightly companion. I am fortunate in finding a young lady of Miss Melpomene's erudition and quality to attend her. I shall await her in my carriage. Please see that she is not further harassed before leaving."

This was said in such tones of confident authority that Forte's shoulders straightened. "Yes, My Lord," he uttered thankfully. "She will be living in London, then?"

The Earl permitted the familiarity, recognizing the old man's real concern. "Yes, with Lady Masterson at Number Three Portman Square. Any mail or *good* wishes may be conveyed to her there." A brief, rather ugly smile touched his lips. "I shall count upon you *not* to furnish this address to your mistress, nor to forward communications which might alarm or sadden the child."

"I quite understand, My Lord," agreed Forte, much relieved.

The Earl of Austell nodded and walked out to his magnificent carriage. Forte did not close the great front door until the visitor was safely within the vehicle. Then he took the liberty of sending a small glass of sherry up to Miss Pommy to drink before she left Highcliff Manor. While he was at it, he took a revivifying sip himself. Miss Pommy! Whatever had she gotten herself into this time?

Three

POMMY HUDDLED in the corner of the Earl's luxurious carriage wishing she had never been born. It had been bad enough to leave Highcliff Manor under the sorrowful and apprehensive gaze of Forte. Worse, Aunt Henga had not deigned to bid her goodbye, nor had Ceci or Lydia, and their deliberate absence merely underlined the conclusion they had expressed about her future status. She was, in addition, most conscious of the threadbare and unfashionable condition of her garments, and was forced to admit that she looked a perfect dowd without even a bonnet to cover her heavy braid of hair.

In contrast, the Earl, who had changed out of his damp clothing before coming to Highcliff to pick her up, looked a pattern card of male elegance from the top of his modish beaver to the tips of his gleaming Hessians. There was a faint hint of spicy fragrance about his person, and his immaculate linen would have gained the approval of Beau Brummell himself. But more than the splendid, strong body, lounging so much at ease beside her in the carriage, more even than his handsome, imperturbable face, the Earl's very presence commanded respect. *He knows who he is,* thought Pommy; *he knows it so completely that he does not need to prove it to anyone in the world.* "I am Austell," he had said, so quietly. Pommy ached with the need to know herself as well.

At the very moment when she had decided miserably that she should never have embarked upon this insane journey, her companion turned his noble head and treated her to a warm and remarkably comforting smile. "We are having a fine adventure, are we not, Miss Melpomene?" he asked. "I anticipate many interesting experiences, and great happiness ahead for you, my child."

"If only your sister will not be put out by your foisting me upon her!" fretted Pommy. "She will take one look at my wretched appearance and think you have brought her a scarecrow!"

Lord Austell laughed easily. "Then shall we deck you out in the latest style before she sees you, little one?" He wondered a little cynically if Miss Rand was already picking up the acquisitive ways of her more fashionable sisters.

Pommy soon set him straight. "No, Milord, *we* shall not! I have better than two pounds which my mother left me, and, before I meet your sister, *I* shall purchase a dress suitable to the rôle of her companion. I only hope," she added grimly, "that she will give me a trial, and not take me in disgust at the outset."

"You have too low an opinion of your worth, Miss Rand," the Earl told her a little sharply. "If you are to go on at all well in Society, you must endeavor to present to the world a more courageous front!"

There was a lengthy silence, broken only by the normal noises of the carriage in motion and its four horses upon the highroad. The Earl, feeling a twinge of quite unaccustomed remorse, was about to speak when Pommy said in a fiercely determined voice, "Milord, you are right! It has only been since I have been living upon the charity of my father's family that I have held myself so cheap! If only your sister had children whom she might wish me to instruct—for I am sound in Greek and competent in Latin. I have also a smattering of poetic German and a little French—just enough to ask directions or order a dinner."

"A veritable Athene!" teased Lord Austell. "Lady Masterson has a son, Gareth, whom she cossets more than I like. Perhaps you may give him a taste for his studies," and he grinned at some private thought.

Pommy, if she had learned anything while living at Highcliff Manor, had discovered that discretion was the only way to self-preservation, so she did not rise to his comments about his young nephew. Better to wait until she had seen the spoiled child before she made promises she might not be able to keep. After all, Lord Austell had hired her to be a companion to an invalid lady, had he not? That much she felt competent to do. She became a little worried when Milord fell into a frowning study. Could it be that he was already regretting his quixotic benevolence in rescuing her from her aunt? Of course! He had saddled himself with a provincial miss, a veritable dowd, and now he was at pains to devise a way to get her into his sister's home without too much embarrassment. Pommy set her shoulders.

"Milord," she began.

"Yes child?" answered the Earl. "What do you wish for now?"

"I wish for nothing, Milord," replied Pommy stiffly, "except to assure you that if, now or at any later date, you find my presence an embarrassment to you, you will kindly tell me so, and I shall arrange to find some other work."

"But I distinctly understood you to say that there was, in fact, no other work for an educated young lady."

"There is always the tavern, which need not be low." Pommy hurried to insert that qualification. "In fact, I have been thinking that I might prove quite useful to a proprietor of a portside inn, where persons from foreign countries could be expected to need an interpreter."

The Earl was regarding her with a look in which amusement and horror were equally blended. "A portside tavern! Miss Melpomene, you cannot realize what you are saying! For one thing, the patrons of such places are invariably Quints and Jibs, or worse, and for another, the number of travelers who would need to be greeted in the Latin tongue could hardly justify the wages your employer would have to pay you."

"You are funning me," Pommy said darkly. "Again."

"What is really worrying you, child?" the Earl asked with a gentleness which would have surprised most of his associates.

Pommy faced him honestly. "I was thinking that you might be regretting having saddled yourself with me, or perhaps you are worrying about my appearance in your sister's fashionable drawing room?"

"There you have hit near the heart of the matter," admitted the Earl. "I must make you an opportunity to spend your two pounds for a suitable dress, and also provide you with a woman to chaperone you at the inns where we shall rest between here and London."

So that was all he had been anxious about! Pommy nodded soberly. "I see the problem. Shall we be going through any sizable towns on this road? Perhaps I might acquire a decent garment in an establishment which caters to companions, ladies' maids, and indigent females."

The Earl glanced sharply at her to see if she were being sarcastic, but met only a clear, guileless, steady look of inquiry.

"There should be opportunities in Exeter, which we should reach late tonight. I feel sure we can find someone to put us in the way of purchasing all you require," he said firmly. He then proceeded to distract her mind from the problem by directing her, in a rhetorical manner, to observe the varied beauties of the country scene. Since it was nearly dusk and still raining heavily, Pommy was forced to chuckle at his raptures, capping them with absurd "appreciations" of her own. A lively contest developed to see which of them could discover the more repulsive example of rural unsightliness to eulogize. This entertained them both for almost an hour.

The Earl was too busy being amused by Pommy's pseudo-enthusiasm for mud-draggled sheep and tumbledown sheds to wonder what freakish impulse had induced a man of his controlled nature and impeccable reputation to offer to escort a deplorably Romantic young female to London in his carriage. To say nothing of sponsoring this country nobody to the position of companion to the exquisite and lachrymose Aurora, Lady Masterson! He could only conclude that it was Boredom, that deadly creeping disease which afflicted the more intelligent of his associates in the *Ton*, which had made him willing to involve himself in the affairs of Miss Melpomene Rand. Damn it! the child was a delight, and honest to a fault! Discounting his own innate chivalry, which had rebelled at the obvious brutality and selfishness of the girl's natural guardians, the Earl wondered whether his pleasure in her freshness and spirit had led him into creating an imbroglio which would embarrass them both. Was he about to stir up a scandal broth in the polite drawing rooms of London's *Haut Ton?* The imperturbable, elusive, untrappable Earl of Austell with a country maiden? He shrugged. It should, he decided, be quite possible for a man of his resources, both social and financial, to handle the business of the Romantic Victim without brouhaha. He found himself grinning. He had not approached any project with this much anticipation for donkey's years! It would be almost a shame when he had her affairs in good order, and would no longer need to put himself out for her!

Four

THEIR GAME of matching rural scenes with inappropriate quotations was summarily interrupted by harsh shouts from both the coachman and the footmen, immediately followed by a jolting stop.

"What the devil—?" snapped the Earl, leaning forward and pulling down the window at his side of the carriage. A single glance was enough to bring him out into the road beside his servants, inspecting a slight body which lay near to the restless hooves of the Earl's highbred horses. Pommy lost no time in climbing down to join them. The Earl was helping his footman to lift the body, which proved to be that of a young woman, and to carry it to the coach.

"Do get in and take hold of her when I lift her up, Melpomene," instructed the Earl. "Place her upon the forward seat. Spread my cloak first—she's dripping with rain and mud."

In a remarkably short time they had the girl safely inside the carriage and were bowling along at a fast pace toward the next village, where the Earl had instructed his coachman to stop at the most presentable inn. Then he turned his attention to his new passenger. Pommy had already wiped the girl's face dry and clean with her best handkerchief, and was smoothing her wet hair gently back from a pallid brow. The Earl drew in his breath sharply. Even in the gloom of the carriage the face had a striking purity, a rare beauty which seemed to radiate light.

Pommy had managed to whip off the wet shawl before she laid the girl on the seat, and had tucked her own warm cloak about the other girl's body. Now she knelt in the swaying vehicle, chafing the cold hands and peering carefully at the blue-white face.

"I think she is hungry, exhausted, and possibly badly frightened," she announced.

The Earl glanced at her. "You keep your head in an emergency, Melpomene," he commended. "Can you infer anything more about our Heroine? Her name and station, perhaps?"

Pommy's glance flew to his enigmatic countenance. With a sinking of heart she thought, *He is mocking me!* and then, *he called* her *the Heroine!* She had no desire to pursue the latter idea; for some reason she dared not acknowledge, it was painful to her. Gathering her pride and her wits to the task, she very carefully examined the face and hands of the rescued girl and said quietly, after a moment:

"She is gently bred. Her hands are soft and free of calluses. Her shoes were expensive; they are well made but not intended for tramping muddy roads. Her stockings are sheer silk, very fine. I do not wish to uncover her to examine her clothing, since she is already chilled, but it is plain her garments are of good quality, in good taste, and suitable for a young woman of fortune. And she is the most beautiful girl I have ever set eyes upon!"

The Earl had been watching her face, rather than the unconscious girl's. "Well done, Pommy! I cannot fault either your judgment or your powers of observation. Nor your heart," he added softly. He sighed. "Well, we shall soon have her in a warm room. Will you continue to care for her?"

"Of course," agreed Pommy stoutly, and wondered why she had been given green eyes, a short, slightly upturned nose, and a mouth too large for the rosebud charm which was the present standard of beauty. Could she ever forget Ceci's mocking chant when first they met as children at a vicarage party? "Green eye, pick a pie, turn around and tell a lie!" And how Lydia had shrieked with laughter?

Fortunately interrupting this unpleasant train of thought came the bustle of their arrival at an inn. It was not long thereafter before the Earl had arranged everything with efficiency and dispatch. The still-unconscious girl had been carried gently to a warm and well-lighted bed chamber; Pommy and the innkeeper's wife had undressed her and installed her in a four-poster with hot bricks to her feet and an extra down comforter around her. Then the good woman hurried off to prepare a hot posset, while the innkeeper sent a manservant to fetch the doctor. Pommy had just finished bathing the face and hands of the unfortunate young woman with hot water, and was drying and gently untangling the long blonde hair, when the Earl entered the room.

"I see you have everything in hand, Pommy," he

remarked, with the rare, warm smile which flustered her senses.

At this moment the girl in the bed stirred, moaned softly, and said, in a breathy small voice, "Where am I? Oh, what has happened to me?"

The Earl came at once to stand beside the bed, but Pommy had already taken the groping slender fingers into her own warm clasp.

"You are in bed in the Turtle's Nest Inn at Belford on the road to London. There is nothing here that can hurt you. I am Pommy Rand, and I will stay with you as long as you wish me to."

The Earl cocked one eyebrow at this masterly assumption of kindly authority. "You put me strongly in mind of my old nanny," he said with a smile. "I daresay it is the best way to handle this rather unconventional situation."

Pommy found she could not meet his teasing eyes. Alas for her tentative dreams! She had been quickly relegated—or had relegated herself—to the position of kindly old nanny to this beautiful girl. *When will it be my turn to be the admired, the beloved?* cried a lonely voice deep within her. Still, there was much satisfaction to be gained from the rôle of ministering angel and Confidante to the Fair Unknown. Pommy squared her shoulders and faced the Earl with a smile whose sturdy sweetness she herself was not aware of.

"We shall do nicely. Mrs. Ainton is bringing a warm posset, and I shall keep our invalid from too much activity until Dr. Stewart has seen her."

"Mrs. Ainton, Dr. Stewart," repeated Lord Austell. "You are quick to pick up the relevant details, Pommy. It appears you would make a good comrade in adversity."

Small comfort, when her secret fantasies had been much different, but Pommy told herself to accept it gratefully. The entrance of Mistress Ainton with the posset helped her to maintain her attitude of cheerful competence. She went to the girl's head and lifted it gently to her own shoulder, supporting the slender frame warmly against her own body.

"Now you must permit good Mrs. Ainton to give you a little nourishment, and soon you will be going on famously," she encouraged.

"You are too kind," murmured the breathy voice, and the big, pale blue eyes sought hers with shy gratitude. "May I know your name? I know you told me, but I—I do not quite remember."

"I am Pommy," she said gently. "Now do not attempt to greet us all in proper form, or we shall be exchanging introductions all evening, and you will not have taken your nourishment before Dr. Stewart arrives!" With a gentle smile she took the spoon from Mrs. Ainton, who was glad to surrender it, and began spooning the hot milk curdled with spiced ale into the invalid's mouth. By the time Dr. Stewart walked into the bedroom, there was a trace of color in the beautiful face, and some animation in the blue eyes.

The Earl, who had been standing in the shadows near the window, came forward quietly and explained what had occurred. Nodding, Dr. Stewart walked to the bed to make his diagnosis. Pommy began to release the girl's hand, but the latter cried out and gripped it tightly, her eyes on the doctor's face.

"Hush now, my dear, you must be very good and quiet, and answer Dr. Stewart's questions, for he cannot decide what is to be done unless you tell him what he needs to know," said Pommy.

The Fair Unknown shed a few tears, which, Pommy observed with strong envy, did not serve to redden her perfect little nose, and then promised to be very good if

45

Pommy would stay beside her and hold her hand. This plan the doctor agreed to, and conducted his examination, both physical and verbal, with gruff kindliness.

A few minutes later he walked over to the Earl and said, "There is really nothing wrong with the young lady which rest and proper diet will not cure. She may of course suffer a slight inflammation of the lungs due to exposure in the storm, but that should not create alarm if reasonable care is taken." He eyed the tall nobleman keenly. "I take it from Ainton's servant that you found the young lady lying in the road?"

"I believe she was running across the road as my carriage approached, and slipped and fell, frightening my horses. They are highbred, and tend to take alarm at the least provocation," the Earl explained by way of apology.

"Women will never understand these matters," said Dr. Stewart. "The gel should have waited to cross the road until you had got past."

"Have you any idea who she may be?" asked the Earl. "The Aintons do not seem to be able to identify her, and my niece has not dared to question her until we had your opinion on her state of health."

Pommy, who had been listening carefully, nodded her head at the Earl's sensible nomination of herself as his niece. He caught her eye at just that moment, surprising her, and a quirk of amusement pulled his lips as he read her unqualified approval of his ploy.

The doctor was speaking. "No, I have never seen the young woman before—and believe me, I would have remembered *that* face! She is a stranger to these parts. I would say a sheltered female, possibly from one of the larger cities, if the ornate quality of her garments is taken into account. Everything silk," he explained, with a conscious smile.

The Earl proffered a fee and profuse thanks for Dr. Stewart's courtesy and dedication in coming out upon such a wretched night. The gentlemen parted with mutual good will, and a jocose comment by Dr. Stewart that if Milord's niece ever chose to become a doctor's assistant, he himself would be delighted to employ her.

"Now *do not,* I beg of you, Pommy," pleaded the Earl when the door had closed after the doctor, "begin to spin out a story in which you accept Stewart's offer, nurse a large family through the cholera, and then die in great agony, surrounded by all your grateful and grieving well-wishers!"

Pommy had to grin at him, thinking as she did so how very well he seemed to understand her, and that no one, not even her beloved grandfather, had ever entered into her fantasies as this man did.

The Earl had come over to the bed, and now was smiling down at the Fair Unknown. "Dr. Stewart gives us a very comfortable report of you, child. Can you rest a little now, while I take Pommy to eat her dinner? She has not had a bite for hours, and is gallantly starving to death in silence!"

This pleasantry caused the perfectly cut lips to form a smile. Slender fingers slowly released their grip on Pommy's warm hand. "Oh, yes, you must refresh yourself, dear Pommy! I shall be content here until you return to me."

"Would you wish to have a maidservant to keep you company?" asked Pommy.

"No!" sighed the invalid. "I shall just wait for you."

The Earl got Pommy out of the room with dispatch. "I have ordered a meal for us in a private parlor. After we have eaten, we must discuss the future of the Fair Unknown, and of yourself."

"However did you know I had designated our charge 'the Fair Unknown'?" asked Pommy, much struck.

"What else?" teased Lord Austell. "I knew *you*, you see."

With an odd little thrill, Pommy scanned the strong, impassive, handsome face above her. The Earl took her arm and escorted her down the passageway to an open door which led to a well-lighted parlor. Spread out upon a table was a splendid dinner, its savory odors steaming up into the air. Pommy was going to sit down when Lord Austell indicated a door leading off to the side.

"In there you will find everything necessary to refresh yourself after our long drive, Pommy. When you are ready, come back and we shall have our dinner."

Pommy had never enjoyed a meal as much as she did that one. Her host was by turns witty and serious, fitting her own moods as though he could sense them. He led her skillfully to discuss a variety of subjects, and seemed to value her opinion. Pommy flowered under such attention as she had never before experienced. Her great green eyes gleamed like emeralds, and her small face was alight with pleasure.

"Have you ever," asked the Earl after a brief silence in which both had been doing yeoman service to the sirloin, "considered releasing your hair from that braid?"

Pommy gave herself to a consideration of the question. "I was used to wear it free over my shoulders, but Aunt Henga said it was messy, and told me to braid it."

"Ah! Aunt Henga again," observed His Lordship. "I think we might use your aunt as a guide line: Whatever she told you to do, we should do the opposite. I find her taste unerringly bad."

Pommy chuckled. "Perhaps I brought out the worst in her? You must admit she presented Ceci very well?"

48

"Ceci—in the brief glimpse I had of her—impressed me as being one who could fend for herself very adequately," commented the Earl. "She has a kittenish charm. Yes, I think Ceci knew from birth how to present her pretty smile and wide brown eyes to best advantage."

" 'Brown-eyed beauty, do your mother's duty,' " quoted Pommy involuntarily. She had heard that rhyme so often quoted by Ceci. At the Earl's quizzical glance, she told him that Ceci had frequently chanted the doggerel at her.

" '*Blue*-eyed beauty' was the way my nanny taught it to me," said the blue-eyed man across the table from her complacently. "It was '*Brown* eye, pick a pie, turn around and tell a lie,' in Nanny's version," he continued, "but I will venture a wager that Ceci told you the thief and liar was green eyed?"

"You would win," Pommy informed him, and laughed. Suddenly the sting was gone forever from that piece of petty malice. She stared at the Earl in such open admiration that a flush came up under his tanned skin.

"You would be well advised not to look at me like that, young Pommy," he warned her. Pommy, experiencing a delicious thrill of excitement, lowered her eyes.

"And now," said the Earl, with the air of one bringing himself firmly back to business, "we must decide on our course of action."

At that moment, Pommy would have agreed to anything the Earl had cared to suggest. "About the Fair Unknown," she nodded.

"About Miss Melpomene Rand, first, and the Fair Unknown as she fits in with those plans," corrected His Lordship. "You may recall," he added sternly, although there was a glow in his eyes as he regarded

49

her, "that we decided you would need refurbishing before we presented you to my sister-in-law. And it was obvious to me that we must also secure some sort of chaperone or at least an abigail for you—for propriety's sake." He overrode her tentative objections. "Lady Masterson's companion must be like Caesar's wife." He looked at her, waiting.

"Above suspicion," she supplied.

They shared a laugh.

"You can have no idea how refreshing it is, after a dozen London Seasons, to encounter a maiden who catches one's literary or scholarly allusions immediately," the Earl told her.

"A dozen? You are chaffing me, unless you wish me to understand that you attended Almack's while still in leading strings." Pommy rallied him.

The color was bright in His Lordship's cheeks, making him look a good deal younger. He said firmly, "To business, little witch. We shall proceed to Exeter tomorrow morning, by which time, I trust, if the good Stewart's diagnosis is correct, our Fair Unknown will be sufficiently restored to travel. Although Exeter is not Paris, or even London, it should be able to supply us with two wardrobes which will pass muster in Town until I can arrange for a dressmaker to wait upon you in Lady Masterson's home." He paused, frowning a little. "I have an idea about our guest. I believe she may be a Londoner running away from something, or someone. She bears the signs of careful upbringing. See if she will confide in you, Pommy. We cannot leave her here in this provincial town without friends or acquaintances or even funds to keep her."

"And she is far too beautiful and helpless to be abandoned," Pommy said softly.

"As you say," agreed His Lordship. "Now I have

arranged that one of the older serving women will sit up with our guest while you sleep, for I cannot have two invalids upon my hands tomorrow, can I?" The Earl neatly countered her protest before Pommy could voice it.

Still Pommy made it. "I said I would sit with her."

"She will be asleep," promised the Earl. "Dr. Stewart gave her a sedative."

In the event, the Earl was proven correct on all counts, for when Pommy entered the bedroom very quietly, it was to behold a motherly female nodding in a rocking chair, a trundle bed set up in a corner, and the Fair Unknown fast asleep in the four-poster. Blessing the Earl, Pommy settled into the cot for the most peaceful slumber she had enjoyed in a long time.

Five

THE EARL'S PARTY made a late start on the following morning. After disposing of a hearty breakfast in bed, the Fair Unknown acknowledged herself recovered from her exposure, and quite fit to travel. She permitted Pommy, now very much aware of time passing, to help her to dress, but then sent for Mrs. Ainton to compliment her upon the quickness with which her laundress had rinsed and dried her guest's muddied clothing.

"For it is most proper to thank those who wait upon one, especially if they render any service outside of the ordinary," she advised Pommy in her sweet breathy voice.

"Our host has been waiting for an hour," Pommy advised *her,* with a little less than perfect charity.

The Beauty still did not move very quickly, though perfectly gracious and willing, and when Pommy finally shepherded her down to the front door, the Earl was discovered pacing back and forth in the sunshine beside his restive team with a rather grim look upon his countenance. Although he cast an enigmatic glance at the Beauty and a quizzical one at Pommy, he did not remark upon their dilatory appearance. Since the score had already been settled, the two females were handed at once into the rear seat while His Lordship elected to place himself on the seat facing, where he could overlook them both without turning.

After about ten minutes of formal silence, Pommy could bear it no longer. "My Lord," she began, "we must first thank you for the really *remarkable forbearance* you displayed in waiting so long for us this morning—"

"True," said the Earl, succinctly.

"But it was my fault," confessed the Fair Unknown. "From some cause or other I can never seem to move at a pace which satisfies anyone else. My papa is wont to say that I drive him to a frenzy, and my dressers are forever leaving in a huff!" Two large tears brimmed over her eyelids and slid down her flawless cheeks. "I am truly sorry for it."

The Earl was regarding her with such alarm that Pommy could not prevent a small chuckle from escaping. That would teach him to give *her* a Look! His own face relaxed into a smile, and he leaned forward to offer the Beauty one of his snowy handkerchieves. While she neatly mopped her face, the Earl sat back and began to talk.

"I have been giving thought to our situation while I waited for you this morning—no, you really must not cry any more, I absolutely forbid it," he said to the Beauty, as two more tears overflowed. "By the way, you must tell us your name. It is too fatiguing to be

53

thinking of you as the Fair Unknown or the Beauty. How are you called?"

"I am Isabelle Boggs," said the girl. "My father is Thomas Boggs, the best vintner in London. I presume you have heard of him?" She peeped at the Earl through lashes two inches long.

"Regularly, once a month," acknowledged the Earl.

"Papa had arranged a match for me with a—minor nobleman in the City. I did not wish to go through with it." She paused, and two more flawless pearls cascaded down her perfect cheeks. "One reason I did not wish for the marriage was that I overheard Alan—he is the minor nobleman of whom I spoke previously, Alan Corcran," Isabelle explained meticulously, "well, as I was saying, I overheard Alan telling a friend of his that I bored him to desperation, and that he, I mean Alan, probably would be forced to be unfaithful to me before the honeymoon was out." She dried the tears from her face. "This conversation took place at the reception my father gave to announce our engagement— mine and Alan's, that is."

Lord Austell was looking as though he began to understand Alan's dilemma, but Pommy was staring with shock and pity at the beautiful girl.

Isabelle caught her glance and said simply, "Alan did not intend anyone but his friend to hear his remark, I am sure. He was speaking quite softly in our entrance hall. I was coming downstairs to the reception. The grand stairway in our home has two bends in it—the servants *loathe* having to clean it—and he, that is, Alan, did not notice my presence. I was a little late, and everyone but Alan and his friend had gone on into the drawing room."

"So you ran away?" asked Pommy, envisioning a frantic, secret flight by night.

"Well, not exactly," Isabelle corrected her. "You see, although I could not really wish to marry a man who was already planning to be unfaithful to me, I had nothing packed and could hardly have fled London at that hour. It was after ten o'clock."

"That should set *you* to rights, my impetuous child," the Earl advised her, *sotto voce*.

Isabelle was going on with her story. "After the reception had ended, I told my father why I did not wish for the connection. He was angry." She sighed, but to the Earl's relief, did not weep again. "He said that I should have told him of my scruples before he had spent all that brass entertaining the *Ton* with best champagne and fine brandies. He refused to consider canceling the arrangements. I told him I would simply not make the responses in church if he forced me to attend the wedding ceremony."

"No wonder you were angry!" cried Pommy, incurably partisan. "Your heart wrung with humiliation, your father obdurate—!"

"Oh, I wasn't angry, exactly," said Isabelle thoughtfully. "I just said no."

The Earl did not bother to hide the mocking grin he sent in Pommy's direction. Feeling a little annoyed, Pommy asked, "Then, if you did not run away, how . . . ?"

"How did I get on the road in the storm? My father packed me off to my aunt in Penzance, to stay until I had accepted his decision." She added, in parenthesis, "That is my Great-aunt Sophronia, not my Aunt Tabitha. I do not like Sophronia, and she dislikes me intensely. I like Tabitha," she concluded, smiling.

"You are fleeing from Great-aunt Sophronia's tyranny?" asked Pommy, hopefully.

"Oh, no! When I got to Penzance, I discovered that

she had caught the measles. Both she and her physician were adamant that I should return to London."

"Could you have not stayed with Aunt Tabitha?" inquired the Earl. "Unless of course she lives in the same house as your Great-aunt Sophronia?"

"Oh, no, Tabitha lives in Bath, and is very much in the social swim there. She would have found me a husband immediately—but not a nobleman. Probably a fortune hunter, Papa says."

Pommy, faint but pursuing, took up the saga. "Then, being forced to return to your papa in London, you were held up by highwaymen who took your coach and forced you to flee for your life?"

"Oh, no!" replied Isabelle kindly.

The Earl gave a snort of laughter, which he disguised by coughing vigorously.

Isabelle was explaining. "My father's horses are not really the finest, more showy than sound, our coachman says. Well, on this return trip to London, first one and then the second developed trouble in their limbs— do not ask me for the particulars, for the groom and coachman were busy quarreling about who should go for help in the storm, and did not bother to explain to me the exact nature of the trouble. Which is probably just as well, for I should not have understood it anyway. I am not," said Isabelle with her dazzling smile, "very bright."

"I am sure you have no need to be, looking as beautiful as you do!" cried Pommy, incorrigibly supportive of the downtrodden.

The Earl's shoulders were shaking, she observed with annoyance, and his blue eyes upon her were full of laughter.

"Let *me* guess," begged the irreverent creature. "You finally got down into the road to settle the argument,

56

since night was coming on and you were cold and hungry? Then, as you made your way to the lee of the coach, where the servants were quarreling, something spooked the horses, and they took off without you. The servants, fearful of their master's wrath on being informed of the loss of his showy but unsound team, took to their heels in pursuit of the runaways. You were, naturally, not best pleased at being abandoned in the middle of nowhere in a pelting storm, so you ran after them. When you beheld us approaching, you tried to wave us down."

Isabelle's beautiful eyes were fixed upon Milord's face with almost worshipful awe. "But it is as though you had been there!" she breathed. "Only I was running in the opposite direction to that taken by the runaway team and the servants. All else is exactly as it occurred!"

The Earl sustained Pommy's scorching glance with aplomb. "Why," he inquired of the vintner's heiress, "did you run in the opposite direction?"

Both her auditors waited while the Beauty considered her answer. "I think," she said breathily at length, "because the wind was behind me, that way. I did not like the rain in my face."

"A rational action," commended the Earl. "As you see, it brought you to us and to safety. I shall send a courier to your papa when we reach Exeter, so that he may not be in a fret at your disappearance."

"Oh, I should not think he would be," answered Isabelle. "He will believe I am still with Great-aunt Sophronia getting my mind changed, for the servants will be reluctant to return to London, even if they should have caught up with the coach, until they have found me."

"You see it is quite simple, Pommy," the Earl advised her with those laughing blue eyes, "and not at all romantical or tragic."

"I am not," agreed Miss Boggs, "Romantic."

It is a shame, thought Pommy in a quite unexplainable depression, *that one who is so perfectly the example of a Heroine should utterly refuse to be Blighted. If only I had her looks,* she thought rebelliously, *I should find a way to*—

At this moment, she caught the Earl's glance upon her, so intent and warmly amused that she knew he was reading her like an open book. A moment later this was verified, for he said softly, "How much more *you* could have made of all this, my dear Pommy! It quite saddens one to consider the wasted opportunities!"

"Do not," said Pommy crossly, "be silly!"

Isabelle joined politely in the Earl's shout of laughter, but rather spoiled the effect by saying, wistfully, "This is how it always is with me! I know something witty has been said, but by the time I have puzzled it out, everyone has stopped laughing. So now I just laugh when the rest do." She sighed. Then, "Was it quite correct of you to call His Lordship 'silly'?" she asked Pommy.

"No, it was not, but he was, so I did," retorted Pommy defiantly, at which the Earl laughed again, and Isabelle, after a bewildered moment, chimed in.

When the Earl's party reached Exeter, the coachman drove them at once to the Angel's Rest, a very grand inn indeed, where ordinary travelers were warned off by the grooms and sent summarily down the street to less important houses. The Earl's party, however, was greeted by Mine Host himself, who hastened to assure His Lordship that His Lordship's servants had arrived the evening before, and that all was prepared, even

58

though His Lordship's delayed arrival had caused considerable consternation.

Completely disregarding this rigmarole, the Earl led his party into the inn and sent his anxiously hovering servants about their various tasks. In the twinkling of an eye, the young ladies were installed in a gracious bedroom, and Milord in the inn's finest, where already fires burned brightly. In a private parlor connecting the two rooms, a tasty collation was quickly set up, and the travelers, not at all weary, were cosseted into forgetting the rigors of their journey. All except Pommy.

"I shall never forget this trip," sighed Pommy, making inroads into a game pie. "It is the most wonderful experience I have yet had!"

Both the Earl and Isabelle looked at her searchingly, for to their possibly jaded taste nothing could have been less attractive than the wretched weather, while the two inns at which they had put up were nothing to the comfort and elegance of London living. Then the Earl's glance softened.

"Pommy has enjoyed traveling in our company," he advised Isabelle softly. "She is paying us an unconscious compliment."

Isabelle nodded, looking vaguely puzzled by accepting the man's judgment.

"I have arranged," began the Earl, "for a dressmaker to wait upon you both in your bedroom within the hour. She will have a seamstress with her, and a number of garments suitable for your consideration. I have also required her to include shoes and all the accessories to a lady's toilette—"

Since both the ladies present were regarding him with surprise mixed with consternation, the Earl adopted his loftiest manner.

"Your father, Miss Boggs, would not fault me for

59

providing his daughter with a suitable costume for her arrival at her home. It would not do at all for you to return home in a bedraggled condition. The servants would be bound to talk." He grinned suddenly. "Do not be stuffy, my dear children! I am finding this whole mad excursion unexpectedly amusing, and I know you would not wish to deny your Benefactor a brief respite from the onerous and solemn duties which are his daily lot."

Miss Isabelle obligingly agreed that *she* would not, for the world! but Pommy cast a wary and incredulous eye upon her benefactor. It was true, he had promised her employment which was unexceptionable, and she knew it, and valued it. If he wished her to present a decorous and suitable appearance before her new employer, it was surely reasonable. Still—!

He caught her rather dubious glance. "That's right, Pommy. You will have to bite the bullet. And you must realize, a girl with your *nous*, that the regimen of a Peer of the Realm is not entirely composed of Romantic flights and primrose dalliance."

"You are doing it again," charged Pommy. "Teasing me." She stared hard at his handsome features, then she smiled reluctantly. "You are a *very* domineering man!"

"But you like it," completed her host, imperturbably.

The dressmaker, when she arrived, proved to exercise a kind of magic. She had been briefed, obviously, for her offerings were exactly what was both suitable and attractive for a young beauty of conservative taste, and for a genteel companion to a great lady. Pommy, eyeing the delicate moss-and-leaf-green materials spread out for her inspection, did not even consider that these might be thought unsuitable. Her chief worry was that they might cost more than the nearly three pounds which she wore in a cloth bag pinned to her chemise. Her concern was soon allayed, as the dressmaker mentioned quite casually that this color was so difficult for the average young lady to wear, that she was most grateful to be getting it off her hands, and named a price for the finished garments which was fortunately within Pommy's budget. If the girl had any fear that she was being subsidized by Lord Austell, this was soon dispelled when the price quoted for the pale blue dress chosen by Isabelle was also extremely modest.

"I must return to this town when next I wish to replenish my wardrobe," Isabelle chirruped, happily. "I swear I have never found such bargains!" and she took the required sum from her reticule, which most fortunately had been hanging from her arm on its cord when she descended from her father's coach the previous day. Since Milord had left after introducing Madame Helene, Pommy was able to follow suit, and the dressmaker, an expatriated Frenchwoman who was awake upon all suits, had nothing but admiration for the English Milord who could keep two such charming females happy in their independence while discharging her own formidable account in private.

Miss Boggs's dress being already made, and the appropriate accessories chosen by both young ladies, Madame's seamstress proceeded to measure Miss Rand for her dress, and promised to set to work upon it at once. "For I know that *ma'amzelle* has need of it by this evening, her own trunks having been lost in the accident," Pommy was told.

As soon as she decently could, Pommy sought out the Earl.

"What is this about an accident?" she queried sharply.

"You are annoyed? I had thought you would be

willing to go along with my *libretto*. You made no demur at being my niece," teased His Lordship.

"Oh, no, you mistake my concern, Lord Austell! I merely wished to know the details of the events I am supposed to have taken part in."

The Earl grinned unrepentantly. "It was really a masterly creation. We were bowling along in the storm, when, on crossing a swollen river, the bridge supports gave way and my carriage was precipitated into the flood. Acting with my usual quickness of wit, I rescued both you and Miss Boggs, but alas, your trunks were beyond even my great strength. The servants," he added meticulously, "rescued themselves. It is only you and Miss Boggs who are very much beholden to me."

Pommy chuckled. "Milord, you are a barefaced fabricator—a worse Romancer than I ever was! Especially when you must know that the host of this inn witnessed our arrival in your own carriage—"

"He had eyes only for the charmingly *déshabillées* young ladies—*neither* of whom could produce a trunk to refute my story!" He smiled. "What difference does it make? We are not even a ten-minutes wonder to these people. Believe me, they have seen many travelers more colorful and less decorous than we! I can only hope Miss Boggs's literal mind will not compel her to deny my *histoire* and make me look all no-how!"

"I should think she will never learn of it," commented Pommy. "She does not seem to be very curious about the affairs of anyone except herself."

"Thank God for that," said the Earl devoutly. "We have still to get you to my sister-in-law without arousing the curiosity of the quizzies!"

Pommy smiled back at him, feeling herself in such perfect charity with this worldly, handsome man as she had never before felt for any human being. She did

62

not stop to consider why she should feel thus about a man she had known a brief two days, and, moreover, one who was as far above her sphere as the very sun in the sky. It was enough that they shared a rather reprehensible sense of humor, and a vivid imagination. Pommy was only grateful for such a comfortable sponsor.

By the exercise of almost unbelievable skill and expedition, Madame's seamstresses delivered to Pommy not one but *two* dresses by eight o'clock that evening. Pommy was able to come into the parlor where the Earl's guests were served, wearing the leaf-green gown, which seemed much more beautiful and modish than she had envisioned it, and made her eyes shine like emeralds. While they were dressing, Isabelle had admired it graciously, and had said with authority:

"My dear Pommy, you must let me dress your hair for you tonight! While your braid is quite suitable for traveling, it will not at all do with that dress! Sit down, now, and hand me your brush!"

Seated before the vanity mirror in the new dress— the finest and most beautiful she had ever owned— Pommy's bemused stare fixed itself upon her image in the mirror, and could hardly accept that the face she saw reflected was her own. Great waves of shining black hair flowed down about her shoulders and almost reached her slender waist, lending interesting shadows to her sparkling eyes, softening her features, and framing the pale creamy face with subtle allure.

"Now I must find some way to catch it up into a becoming coiffure," Isabelle said.

Pommy watched, fascinated, as the other girl brought beauty out of what had always appeared to her to be her unrelieved plainness. When she tried to express her gratitude, Isabelle brushed it aside calmly. "I had an excellent governess," she said. "While Miss Pomfrit frequently told me she could do nothing to enlighten my ignorance in intellectual matters, she did admit that I had a rare knack with the more social graces—except conversation."

In honor of his guests, the Earl had dressed for dinner. When Pommy beheld him in his black and silver grandeur, her breath caught and her green eyes widened. Though appearing perfectly relaxed and at his ease, he succeeded in giving the meal a delightfully festive atmosphere. He did not seem to single Pommy out, being most correct in his attentions to both of his guests, yet several times Pommy caught his bright blue gaze intently fixed upon her, and hoped he was a little pleased at the swan Isabelle had created from the ugly duckling. She found it difficult to keep her own eyes off the austere magnificence of his costume, admiring how faultlessly it fitted him, and how well the somber colors became his strong features and his black hair, which he wore unpowdered after the new fashion. Pommy thought she had never seen so impressive a man in her life, for the obese, casual Squire Rand had scorned fine apparel, often saying he was glad he was no jumped-up popinjay, or Town Beau! Her grandfather had dressed as befitted his position, and the professional men in the district—Dr. Mannering and Lawyer Morris—were always soberly clad. The Earl, therefore, seemed to her like a being from a different sphere, and she looked at him with awe and admiration.

When the ladies rose at the end of the meal, Milord rose with them.

"Shall we not leave you to your wine, My Lord?" asked Isabelle, correctly.

"Since you have nowhere to retire to save your bedroom, will you not favor me by remaining here in the parlor for half an hour? There is nothing I should rather do than converse with you!" invited His Lordship.

Pommy gladly took a chair he indicated before the fire, and Isabelle, a little more hesitant, allowed herself to be persuaded also. As it happened, however, the other two found Miss Boggs to be an inhibitor of sprightly conversation, as she had warned them earlier. After a rather labored half hour, she rose to retire to her room, and Pommy almost thankfully prepared to follow her.

As she reached the doorway through which Isabelle had passed just a moment earlier, the Earl said authoritatively, "I wish you to remain here for ten minutes, Pommy! There is a matter of business I must discuss with you."

Isabelle turned her head back over one perfect shoulder and nodded at Pommy encouragingly. "You must not be making company of me," she said with gentle dignity. "I am sure you have family matters to be considered."

Pommy went back to her chair with almost a feeling of relief. The Earl closed the door and joined her.

"Now!" he said, on a breath, "we can be comfortable."

Pommy dimpled up at him. "She is so lovely to look at, she doesn't need to speak," she excused.

"As her reluctant swain admitted, she is boring," fumed the Earl. "That air of bland expectance with which she awaits one's next words quite dries up the springs of conversation! Now we must plan for your meeting with Lady Masterson. First, immediately after reaching London, we shall restore Miss Boggs to her father. Both of us together, I think, so he will not get the idea I have been squiring his daughter unchaperoned through the countryside. Even if pressed, we shall *not* stay for tea. We shall go at once to Lady Masterson's residence. I sent off a groom before dinner tonight, to ride ahead of us and inform Her Ladyship that I have found the perfect companion, whom I am bringing, together with her friend who is returning to her home in London. That should take care of *les convenances* adequately, don't you agree?"

"It is Masterly," smiled Pommy. "It is obvious to me that you have a remarkable degree of skill in dealing with—ah—*les convenances,* Milord!"

"You would imply, circumventing them, madame?" queried her host, settling comfortably into his chair and grinning at her.

"Practice makes perfect, I have no doubt," suggested Pommy, greatly daring. Though she knew herself to be quite out of his class in every way, she could not resist responding to the challenge in those bright blue eyes.

"Devil!" said His Lordship, lazily, stretching out his arm for the decanter upon the side table near him. "Will you have a sip of sherry with me, Pommy?"

"Whatever you wish," agreed Pommy, her unsophisticated heart in her eyes.

Without haste, Milord poured two glasses, one full, the other a token. Handing her the latter, he raised his glass to her. "To the metamorphosis of Melpomene," he toasted.

"Ugly Duckling into Swan?" the girl suggested, laughing happily. "You must give Isabelle credit for accomplished fingers. I am sure I have never looked so well."

"And what Romantic imaginings has your newly discovered beauty brought to mind?"

Pommy pondered. "Why, none, sir. I suppose I believe that the new look Isabelle has given me is itself a fantasy—and tomorrow I shall be the same Pommy as ever."

"There could be worse fates," said the Earl, tossing

off his sherry. He rose and extended his hand. "Off with you, infant! You must get your rest before we attempt another day on the highroad."

Pommy rose and faced him, her sherry still untouched. "May I not propose a toast to you, Milord?" she asked shyly.

The big man looked down at her somberly. "No, child, I think not. With the addition of our prosaic companion, the magic has gone out of our Odyssey. Drink up and say good night."

Sherry had never tasted so bitter to the girl as at that moment.

He was closing a door, and she knew he was wise to do so, for there was no place on the other side of it for Pommy Rand.

Six

THE REST of the journey was as dull as the Earl had
predicted. They rode in great comfort, and stopped
frequently for refreshment and rest, but Lord Austell,
for all his perfect address, behaved like a man doing
his duty, while Isabelle was a boring companion in
spite of her sweetness of nature. Pommy was actually
pleased when they finally deposited Miss Boggs at her
father's ornate mansion in Thornapple Square. Boggs,
initially inclined to be suspicious of his daughter's
unexpected appearance with two strangers, became too
obsequious upon learning the name and style of his
daughter's rescuer. The Earl refused the vintner's hearty
invitation to take pot luck and they left with Isabelle's
tearful urgings that Pommy call soon to see her ring-
ing in their ears.

The drive to Portman Square was marked by a
silence which Pommy found painful but impossible to

break. Of course His Lordship was bored and wishing he had never involved himself in so much Samaritanism! Two hapless females to be rescued from the results of their own folly! No wonder he was wishing *himself* quit of the whole wretched business, and *herself* in Jericho, rather than Portman Square! Setting her small chin firmly, she used the time to consider a plan of action.

You must begin as you intend to go on, she told herself. *No flights of fancy, no Romantic imaginings. You will do your best to entertain and console the weeping widow, you will be tireless in her service, sparing no attentions.* And if this program seemed to offer little pleasure, Pommy accepted it solemnly. No matter that she would be, as always, on the outer fringe of the fun, watching others enjoy themselves, while she dwindled into an ape-leader, an old crone—companion!—she hastily corrected herself. Perhaps, if he thought of her at all, the Earl would be grateful for her devoted service to his widowed sister. She sighed involuntarily.

The Earl turned to her with a quizzical smile and spoke at last.

"Courage, Pommy! Aurora's wail is worse than her behavior. I am hoping that you will bring both laughter and good common sense into my sister-in-law's *ménage.* The Lady Masterson feeds upon melancholy, but she has a sweet and generous nature. She was quite a different person when my brother was alive. Since his death, however, she appears to have felt it her duty to wither away in a series of imagined illnesses. I shall expect you to restore her to a more wholesome view of life."

Pommy looked appalled at the task.

The Earl laughed for the first time that day. "Just involve her and her household in some of your Romantic adventures. I promise to pull you out of them if the consequences threaten to become disastrous!"

And then they were at Number Three Portman Square.

As Milord led her into the imposing mansion, where the butler was bowing almost to his knees, and the footmen stood rigid in their powdered wigs and livery, Pommy could only be thankful for her new moss-green gown and the charming little bonnet which had materialized with it. At least she need not meet this formidable dowager, with her vapors and megrims, in a dowdy dress!

"You may tell Lady Masterson we are here, Mikkle."

"She is awaiting you, My Lord," smiled the butler. "If you will follow me?"

When they were shown into Milady's drawing room, it was to see a bright fire, masses of fragrant flowers out of season, and furnishings of the most feminine elegance. Pommy peered around apprehensively for the imaginery invalid, only to find herself facing a tiny, delicate beauty with white-gold hair and huge sad gray eyes set like silver in a lovely face.

"Aurora, my dear," began the Earl briskly, bending over her fragile, bejewelled white hand, "may I present to you Miss Melpomene Rand of whom I wrote you, who has come all the way from Cornwall, through great vicissitudes and hazards, to bear you company? Miss Rand," he took her hand and led her to his hostess, "this is my sister-in-law, Aurora, Lady Masterson."

The tiny sparkling hand was extended to her, and Pommy found herself curtseying as though her hostess were Royalty.

This gesture seemed to please Milady. "So good of you to come," said Her Ladyship in a voice as sweetly plangent as a chime of silver bells. "Did you have a wretched journey, my poor child?"

Pommy, incurably honest, found that she could not mouth the conventional nothings. *You must begin as you intend to go on,* she had told herself in the Earl's carriage. *If you are true to yourself, you cannot be exposed as a fraud.* She lifted her chin and said what she felt.

"Oh, no, Milady! I have never gone upon a journey I enjoyed as greatly! The Earl is so lighthearted and amusing. He is forever funning! Such very good company!"

The invalid raised her shadowed gray eyes in startled inquiry to scan Lord Austell's imperturbable face.

"Can we be speaking of the same Earl?" demanded the Lady Masterson in anything but bell-like tones.

The Earl's shout of laughter reverberated through the room. "I told you she would startle you out of the megrims," he chuckled. "Now do offer us a cup of tea, Aurora. We have just delivered Melpomene's traveling companion to her father, and I need a restorative. I charge you," he added, with the teasing smile Pommy adored, "to make Pommy tell you about the beautiful Miss Boggs. It will give you something to laugh about, I promise you!"

Whether it was because of the Earl's charm and virility, or the interest caused by Pommy's arrival, the Lady Masterson brightened perceptibly as the afternoon progressed. Tea was accompanied by salvers of the most delicious pastries Pommy had ever tasted, and she did them full justice. At one point Lord Austell chuckled. Pommy, lifting her eyes, perceived Lady Masterson was watching her in fascination. Pommy smiled wryly.

"I am making a pig of myself, am I not? I must admit

71

that such cakes as these have never come in my way before. I think they must be what are called Angel Food, are they not, My Lady? For surely they are heavenly morsels."

Lady Masterson found herself smiling back at the child. Really, she wondered, what had Derek brought to her? The girl was plainly a country cousin, yet voice and accent evidenced breeding. Her manners were impeccable; for all her relish of the sweets, she ate daintily. And her family had treated her cruelly, if Derek's letter could be believed. A new thought struck Lady Masterson. Could Derek be *interested*? It hardly seemed possible, after all the wasted efforts of the matchmaking mamas and frustrated débutantes, many of them quite acceptable as to Family, and some of them great heiresses as well. Of course Derek had no need to marry money, nor any particular reason to ally his House with another equally noble. Yet he was sponsoring this child with a zest his sister-in-law had no difficulty in discerning. The girl was a nobody. Surely her high-in-the-instep brother would not be considering such an alliance?

Agog with curiosity, Aurora decided to sit up for dinner that evening, instead of taking it in her bedroom as had become her custom.

While Pommy, urged by the Earl, was selecting a final *patisserie*, Her Ladyship bent toward him and said in an undertone, "I insist that you remain to dine with me tonight, to launch your protégée. Perhaps you may even find occasion to display some of the light-hearted good humor the child is so enthusiastic about."

"My dear Aurora," the Earl said lazily, "it is my understanding that you rarely stay downstairs for dinner. Can it be that my prescription has already been of benefit? Believe me, she will continue to delight you."

Aurora stared at him. His face was alight with laughter and his bright blue eyes were showing more warmth than she remembered since his younger brother died. At once she required him to pull the bell rope, and when the butler presented himself, she informed him that His Lordship would be staying for dinner, and that she herself and Miss Rand would have it with him in the dining room. She was just asking Mikkle whether Mr. Gareth was to dine with them, when a tall young exquisite strolled into the drawing room and stared at the persons seated there out of silver-gray, black-lashed eyes exactly like Lady Masterson's.

Pommy swallowed a gulp of surprise. She had never seen so flawless a human being in her life. Even the beautiful Isabelle's luster was paled before the bright effulgence of this youth's splendor.

Acknowledging a reaction she had seen many times before, Lady Masterson smiled proudly and announced, "Miss Rand, may I present my son Gareth?"

The man's well-cut lips softened into a delightful smile. "Miss Rand! A pleasure to meet you, Ma'am." He bowed over her hand, and Pommy was not surprised to note that his every action was graceful yet manly.

The Nonpareil turned to his mother. "I am happy to see you in such high spirits, Mama," he said, kissing her hand and then her cheek. "Uncle Derek, this is a pleasure we have too seldom! You are looking well, sir. Are you back in Town to stay?"

The two men shook hands, and the Earl's smile was cordial. It was evident that he liked his heir. "I believe I shall find enough to keep me interested for a little while, Gareth. I plan a rather longer stay in London than usual. For one thing, I have brought your mother a companion—Miss Melpomene Rand, whose grandfa-

73

ther was the Reverend Augustus Mayo, one of our great scholars."

"Oh!" Gareth said, smiling amiably. "Are you also a scholar, Miss Rand?"

"Oh, no, sir," Pommy hastened to disclaim. "I have neither the wisdom nor the training."

Both Lady Masterson and her son seemed to find this modesty admirable, and Gareth even sighed in relief. "I was beginning to be in a quake lest I should find myself exposing my deficiencies! At Eton I was forever running into difficulties with my tutors." He chuckled. "They were wont to say that I had more bottom than brains!"

His mother proudly interpreted. "Like his dear father, Gareth excels in all the manly sports. He is a bruising rider who never refuses any hazard, I am told. Of course, he has no head for figures, but that is not at all necessary when dear Derek has instructed his comptroller to handle all our affairs for us." She cast her brother-in-law a grateful look, and then summoned Mikkle again, requiring him to get the housekeeper to escort Miss Rand to her room.

"Go now, child, and let Mrs. Upton send a maid to assist you in dressing for dinner. Gareth, you may leave us also. I have matters to discuss with your uncle."

When the two young people had gone, the Earl rattled in before his sister-in-law could begin the inquisition she clearly intended.

"Something is troubling Gareth." It was a statement rather than a question.

The widow shrugged an exquisite shoulder, and would not meet his eyes. "Oh, it is some boyish whim! Gareth is moody, you know."

"Gareth is one-and-twenty—*not* a boy, Aurora! Is he pining to go to his estate?"

Lady Masterson put on a lachrymose expression and took out a lace-edged scrap of handkerchief. "You know he is like a child, forever wishing to race in the fields and climb trees and shoot and ride horses—and dogs—"

"Hardly dogs, my dear Aurora, but I catch your meaning. Gareth has the soul and the interests of an English squire, and will make an excellent husbandman of his lands, for all his elegance of person and the Town bronze you have succeeded in giving him. Aurora—let the lad go! He will never leave your side as long as you hold him with you. He tries to please you, but he is truly miserable among the Beaux and the Corinthians. Free him to embrace his heritage! It is what his father would have desired."

"Have you forgotten that it was that very heritage which took his father's life? He would be with us today if he had not saved that herdsman's child from the bull!"

"It was an act of heroism," the Earl said gently. "He could not have done otherwise."

Lady Masterson turned the conversation quickly. "I must thank you for your efforts to find me a companion," she said, rallying him a little archly. "Am I to suppose that you have a special interest in—the scholar's grandchild?"

The Earl looked sober. "Why, I suppose I must have," he admitted. "I think it was her gallantry in her wretched situation which impressed me. And then she is so *Romantic*—!" he chuckled, his eyes soft.

Lady Masterson was amazed. This was more serious than she had thought. Prudently she decided to say no more upon this head until she had taken the child's measure. At least she was a gentlewoman, and soft voiced, and she was young enough to be biddable. But as a wife for the Earl of Austell?

To her credit, Lady Masterson felt neither alarm nor jealousy at the thought that His Lordship might be intending to marry and provide his vast estates with an heir of his own body. She had more than enough in her lavish widow's portion and her inheritance from her own father, an eccentric duke who was never seen without a posy in his hatband. Gareth's small estate, which he had from his father, and his allowance from the Earl, would ensure that money would never be a problem to him. Her interest in Miss Rand was solely motivated by a fear that the child would not prove a suitable chatelaine for the two great mansions and the lavish Town house which were His Lordship's possessions. For the girl was no beauty, and her background, while decent, was not impressive in any way.

During dinner, which was for some reason more amusing than any she had bothered to attend of late, she had ample opportunity to behold the side of the Earl which Pommy had praised. Derek's humor was jovial; he made sly jokes, laughed frequently, and challenged Miss Rand into making a dozen witty observations on their journey. The girl was obviously smitten. Of the Earl's feelings she could not be so certain: His smile was warm, and his eyes, when they rested on the girl, were alight with interest. But he must be nearly twenty years the child's senior. Yes, there was much for Aurora to do! And the first thing would be to take the girl to her own dressmaker tomorrow—for it must never be said that Aurora Masterson's companion was a dowd!

When Her Ladyship made the announcement, not at all àpropos of anything which was being said, that she intended to introduce Miss Rand to the fashionable shops the following day, the Earl hid a smile, Pommy's eyes sparkled with pleasure, and Gareth looked apprehensive.

"I have an appointment with some of my friends at Manton's, Mother. I fear I shall not be able to—"

"Nonsense, Gareth, I do not at all wish to have you accompany us," she said indulgently. "Your taste is not as good as your uncle's. Now if *he* were to offer to come—" and she raised a mischievous eyebrow at the Earl, waiting to see him squirm out of the invitation. To her shocked surprise, Derek agreed at once to come, saying, with a challenging smile, "When do you wish me to call for you, my dear Aurora?"

By the time the details of the expedition had been settled, Lady Masterson felt almost breathless. Lord Austell was smiling imperturbably, and Pommy was pink with pleasure.

Seven

WHEN POMMY AWOKE, she could not at first accept her luxurious surroundings as actual, and thought that she must still be in some sort of dream. Then the memory of the events of the previous day rushed into her mind, and she scrambled out of bed to examine, in the daylight, the charming room she had been almost too weary to take in the night before. It was a charming bedroom, all greens and blues and rich soft fabrics and mirrors. Mirrors! Half a dozen of them, including the first full-length one Pommy had ever seen. She ran to stand in front of it, chuckling at the sight of the tousle-haired girl who stared back at her with wide laughing eyes. Pommy hugged herself in glee.

"Even if Lady Masterson permits me to stay only a few days, it will be worth it! This is the bower of a princess. Oh, how lucky I am to be in it!"

Pulling her voluminous cotton nightgown, a hand-me-down from Aunt Henga, around her in what she considered to be a fashionable drape, Pommy walked back and forth in front of the mirror, eyes on her peacocking image.

Then she laughed aloud, and strolled around the spacious room, enjoying all the pretty and elegant furnishings. It was while she was so employed that a discreet knock sounded upon the door. Without waiting for an answer, a very capable-looking middle-aged woman in a dark blue uniform entered and greeted Pommy with surprise and a little censure.

"Oh, you are waking, Miss! I am Gordon, Lady M.'s dresser. I had not thought to find you up!"

"I have not yet learned to keep Town hours, you see," confessed Pommy, smiling.

She could not know how young she looked, in the huge nightgown, her splendid mane of shining black hair tumbling down almost to her waist, her huge green eyes sparkling with excitement, her small piquant face alight. Lady Masterson's dresser revised the intentions with which she had entered the room. She had come expecting to find a country bumpkin, a puffed-up little provincial, all presumption and push, who would disrupt the well-ordered routine of Milady's house and create Problems, being neither true Quality nor actual menial. Instead she discovered an artless child, eager to share her delight in the unaccustomed luxury. No pretensions here which must be depressed, admitted Gordon, a martinet in the Servants' Hall and so conscious of her role as Milady's dresser as to have won the soubriquet "The Dragon." Almost against her will her expression softened.

"Now then, Miss Rand, we must get you dressed an' ready to go down to breakfast. For you will not wish it brought to you here, I think?"

Pommy looked appalled. "Oh no, ma'am! I have never had breakfast in bed—well, once, when I had the mumps, they left a tray inside my door, not wishing to catch the disease themselves, you see—"

"There will be nothing like that here," Gordon assured her, with sublime confidence that an All-Wise Deity would not permit encroaching infections to disrupt Lady Masterson's *ménage*. "Now, Miss Rand—"

"Oh," interrupted Pommy urgently, "must you call me that? I know it is my name, but—but Pommy is more friendly!" she ended in a rush.

Gordon scrutinized the pleading face. Of course! Like a fish out of water in this grand household, the child was anxious for a guiding hand. Had she but known, Pommy could not have chosen a more acceptable approach.

The Dragon's smile would not have been recognized in the Servants' Hall. "Well, Miss, you must admit your given name is a mouthful."

"Melpomene?" The girl sighed. "The *trouble* that name has caused me! But Pommy is not hard to say . . . if you please?"

Gordon smiled indulgently. "Very well, Miss Pommy. Now let me see your wardrobe, and we shall have you ready for your breakfast in the twinkling of a bed post!"

Nothing could have cemented the good relationship Pommy was establishing with the Dragon as well as what the girl did now. She hurried to the elegant armoire in which she had hung her two new dresses and the best two of her former wardrobe—all she had brought from Highcliff Manor. Both of these were years out of style—if indeed they had ever been in it—and well worn from many washings. The pitiful accessories, darned stockings, mended undergarments, were displayed in a small heap on the floor of the armoire, for Pommy had been too sleepy to look out a better place last night. But instead of showing embarrassment, or asking for pity, Pommy displayed the two new dresses with pride.

"I have this silk one for dressing up, and this pretty woolen one for everyday. There is even a bonnet to match it!"

The pride in the girl's face as she displayed her meager wardrobe did something to Gordon's well-armored heart. Then, noting the newness and the alamodality of the two costumes, she wondered sharply if Lord Austell had . . .

The child made her regret her suspicions before she had completely framed them.

"These may not be up to standards, but you see I had just two pounds to spend—in my home village a veritable fortune!—and we must remember that I have not come to London to make a fashionable début, Miss Gordon!" She chuckled at her own jest.

"You must call me just 'Gordon,' Miss Pommy. Your dresses are very pretty and suitable, but you will have need of more than two if you are to be Lady Masterson's companion. I have no doubt she will arrange for a wardrobe for you. No," she correctly identified the look on the girl's face, "it will not be charity, for of course you are to receive a wage, as is customary." To put an end to argument, Gordon said with the brisk hauteur of the superior dresser who knows both her own worth and her job, "Now you must wash your face and hands, Miss Pommy, and put on the woolen dress. I shall return to assist you with your hair in ten minutes."

Half an hour later, Pommy, directed by Mikkle, entered the breakfast room. She was feeling complacent. Her new dress looked very well; it had apparently been freshened and pressed while she was wearing the evening gown the night before. Also Gordon had proved an even more accomplished *coiffeuse* than Isabelle ever was.

Gareth was already seated at the table, somberly addressing his breakfast. He rose and held her chair for her, naming the contents of several silver dishes set over candles to keep warm. Pommy chose some from each, which so put Gareth in charity with her that he smiled for the first time. Pommy began to eat without bothering him by inane inquiries into his health, or vapid chatter about the weather. This restraint at first surprised and then impressed him, and a little of the tension went out of his shoulders. After a silent five minutes dedicated to the absorption of food, Gareth touched his lips with a snowy napkin and asked Pommy if he could pour her a cup of coffee.

"I am sure it should be my office to pour yours, sir," the girl said with a smile, suiting action to word.

When she handed her host a cup and gave herself one, Gareth said thoughtfully, "You are very quiet, are you not?" Then, lest his comment had offended her, he added simply, "I like it."

Pommy stirred cream into the coffee. "Thank you. My uncle could never bear gabble-mongering, as he called it, at the breakfast table, so I got into the habit of silence at that time."

"Lady Jersey is called 'Silence,' " said Gareth moodily, "but that is because she is forever talking." His beautiful countenance expressed such intense dissatisfaction that Pommy wondered, first, if he disliked Lady Jersey, then second, if he disliked company at the breakfast table. This consideration so troubled her that, finishing her slice of ham in two bites, she asked gently, "Shall I go now, Gareth? Do you prefer to break your fast alone? Mikkle directed me here today, but I promise I shan't bother you another morning! Word of honor!"

Gareth stared at her in startled inquiry. "Good God, Miss Rand! I find your company particularly soothing, as a matter of fact. No, if I have been scowling it is because the thought of Lady Jersey's endless conversation reminded me how much I dislike the whole social crush."

"You dislike it? Then why—?" Pommy caught herself up. She had no business asking her host for explanations.

But Gareth was apparently eager to confide in his new acquaintance.

"Then why do I stay in London, enduring a silly, wasteful, boring existence, when my estates are crying out for my supervision? You may well wonder at it, Miss Rand! I do myself, twenty times a day!" he concluded with a bitterness which startled Pommy. She decided he must be unhappy indeed, if he would so freely confide in one who was, after all, a comparative stranger. With a sympathetic desire to help, she asked softly:

"Where are they—your estates, Gareth?"

As she had hoped, this simple question set him off on a lengthy and enthusiastic description of his patrimony—its location, acreage, resources, natural beauties—which included a trout stream, a lake large enough for boating and swimming, and woods well supplied with game. "And when I tell you," he concluded, with a sudden reversion to his former depression, "that we have also a very respectable hunt-club forming in the district—oh, it is not The Quorn, I grant you, but the members are all friends of mine, and very keen!—you will see that going to stupid balls and routs and trying to talk with chattering débutantes and old quizzies is *not* what I would choose to be doing!"

"Then why not leave?" asked Pommy logically.

"Mother!" groaned Gareth.

"Oh," said Pommy. "I—I see."

"I am the worst beast in Nature," Gareth castigated himself. "Mother is so lonely since my father was killed, so fearful of my leaving her, that I have not the heart—" He paused.

Pommy's own heart warmed to this responsible son. "Of course you have not felt that leaving her was the thing," she agreed gently. "But the situation has changed, has it not? Lady Masterson now has a companion—and while I am not in any way a substitute for yourself, still I shall do all in my power to amuse and assist her. So might not this be your opportunity to visit your estates, at least briefly?"

Gareth had been looking more cheerful as she spoke, but after a few minutes thought, he sighed deeply and shook his head.

"I cannot tell you how much I appreciate your kindness, Miss Rand, but it will not do! You see, one of Mama's most frequent remarks is to the effect that she is so *grateful* to have my presence, since she needs a man's strong arm to lean upon."

"Does she go into Society, then?" queried Pommy. "I had thought, from what Lord Austell said, that she was much at home."

"Oh, she is!" agreed her son gloomily. "She is still invited everywhere, for you must know that she and my father were a very welcome couple at every kind of social event, for they were the merriest pair!" He sighed again. "It quite breaks my heart to see her so languid and—and—tearful!" he concluded gruffly.

Pommy felt something rising in her breast which was certainly not sympathy. It was anger, and it was directed at the Lady Masterson, her new mistress. How could she keep this splendid considerate son of hers on a leading string, like a small child or—or a *puppy,* to amuse and comfort her! Could she not see that she was making him very unhappy? As always happened when she was strongly moved, Pommy began to fantasize some possible solutions to the problem. The first that came to her mind was a substitute. The Lady Masterson, even at her advanced age—for she must be all of thirty-eight or thirty-nine—was still an exceedingly beautiful woman, when she forgot her lachrymose ways. "I understand from Lord Austell," she said offhandedly, "that he intended to remain for most of the Season in London. Surely he would act as his sister-in-law's escort and—uh—strong arm?"

"By Jove, Miss Pommy," said Gareth, suddenly appearing hopeful, "you may have something! I myself heard him say he intended a longer stay than usual in the City. Perhaps, a little later, when Mama is engaged with you and with the Earl, I might just slip away—"

It was said so wistfully that Pommy at once vowed she would find some way to help this beautiful youth to the very proper enjoyment of his own estates.

Eight

GARETH and Pommy were just getting up from the table when a maid entered the room to inform Miss Rand that Her Ladyship had decided to rise at the unheard-of hour of nine o'clock in order to take Miss Rand to see Lady Masterson's dressmaker, and would appreciate Miss Rand being ready to go out by eleven.

"Oh, but surely—this is an imposition!" cried Pommy, much distressed by the notion of disrupting the widow's morning routine.

Gareth, on the other hand, was looking remarkably pleased. "Do you not see, Pommy, it is just as you said! She is *interested!* She was used to love clothes so, and was considered the best-dressed woman in the *Beau Monde*. It could not be better!"

Pommy reluctantly agreed, noting that the young man had called her Pommy in his excitement. Perhaps it was all for the best, and she must sink her pride and accept whatever good the gods and Lady Masterson were pleased to bestow upon her. But there was one thing she must get clear now, whilst she had Gareth with her.

"What is the stipend paid to a companion?" she asked.

Gareth stared. "Why—er—I really have no idea," he answered slowly. "Perhaps one hundred pounds a year?"

Pommy broke into joyous laughter. "It is easily seen, sir, that *you* have never hired a companion! *One hundred pounds!* You might as well say one thousand!"

Gareth's beautiful mouth widened in a sheepish grin. "Is it too much, then? Well, I am sure I do not know."

"Then you should have said so at the outset, and not led the poor companion into dreams far above her station," Pommy teased.

The young man regarded her doubtfully, then laughed. "You are bamming me, are you not? No one has ever done so since I came to Town. I was used to have several friends who were forever cracking wits with me," he finished wistfully.

"Then you may expect more of the same while I am here," Pommy replied firmly. It was her private opinion that the youth was far too solemn for his age. It was clearly her duty to rouse him, as well as his melancholy parent, to a realization of the joy to be found in small jokes.

When he went off for his daily ride in the Park, Pommy ran lightly upstairs to her pretty room to don the bonnet which went with the woolen dress. As she took up her reticule and the gloves she had always worn to church, Pommy felt that she was armored to face whatever Fate might bring.

What Fate sent was the Earl, looking more splendid in his formal morning costume than she had yet been privileged to behold him. In fact her eyes and mouth rounded into "O's" at sight of his sartorial magnificence. The Earl noted this manifestation with a boyish grin.

"Oh, Pommy, you are a refreshment and a delight! You cannot expect me to believe that your open-mouthed admiration is not a put-on! Having been exposed to Gareth's alamodality, as organized by his mother, you must surely assess my claims as paltry!"

A sudden, and to Pommy, unwelcome blush stained the girl's cheeks. The Earl noted this sign with amusement, and would no doubt have continued in the same vein had not Lady Masterson entered at that moment, accompanied by Gordon and two maidservants holding various accessories without which Milady apparently deemed it impossible to venture from her home.

The Earl took immediate and good-natured charge of the situation, removing the two parasols between which she could not decide ("My carriage is *covered,* dear Aurora!"), the second and larger of the two reticules ("You do remember you agreed to permit *me* to stand the nonsense today!"), and the fur muff ("Really, Aurora, this is too much! We are not venturing into Polar regions this morning!").

Pommy, accustomed to the Rand family's constant contentiousness, was greatly surprised to see how cheerfully Lady Masterson reacted to the Earl's masterful behavior. Her Ladyship did not appear to find it odd that the gentleman should take over their shopping expedition so cavalierly; in fact she accepted it with the complacent enjoyment of a stroked kitten. It became plain to Pommy that it would be sensible to secure a worldly-wise, strong-minded, and well-to-pass partner for Lady Masterson, since she clearly forgot her melancholy while in the company of such a gentleman. Lord Austell would seem to be the obvious choice, for he was available, acceptable to the lady, and satisfied all requirements. Pommy found herself reluctant, for no reason she could discover, to promote this decidedly suitable match. And for once she did not try to fantasize the course of events which would follow a declaration from the Earl to Lady Masterson. In fact, she suddenly felt quite out of sorts with herself and her two gaily chatting companions, and wondered if this wave of loneliness which threatened to swamp her spirits and cut up her peace would be her habitual mood as Lady Masterson's companion. Contrasting this trip in the Earl's carriage with her first day's ride from Sayre Village, she recalled her naive pleasure in the Earl's attention, and their shared laughter, and could almost find it in her heart to resent her employer's presence. Then, disgusted with her own petty ingratitude, she resolutely turned her attention to the light banter of her fellow-passengers, and assumed an attentive yet properly respectful demeanor.

When they reached the establishment of Mlle. Lutetie, the Earl offered each of the ladies an arm, and when Pommy would have held back, he gave her such a quelling glance that she hastily put her fingers upon his sleeve.

The salon was decorated with gold-framed mirrors and beautiful gold and crystal chandeliers whose lusters sparkled like diamonds in the light of their candles. A thick carpet covered the floor, flowers were displayed in large bowls, and an exotic drift of perfume sweetened the air. Pommy drew in a long breath.

"It's gorgeous," she whispered, "but where are the dresses?"

For some reason this set both her companions to laughing. It was a jovial group which presented itself to the other patrons and the proprietress of the salon.

Mlle. Lutetie hurried toward them, her attitude that of a sharp business woman under the veneer of Gallic enthusiasm with which she greeted these important clients. While she was arranging chairs for Lady Masterson and Pommy, the Earl, casting a harassed look at the stylishly dressed ladies in the room, suddenly announced that an urgent appointment, till this instant forgotten, would compel him to leave them to their delicate negotiations. He promised to return in two hours to drive them home, or through the Park if they would so honor him.

"Nonsense, Derek," said Lady Masterson astringently. "You are either bored or terrified at the notion of having to talk about female garments for two hours." At his rueful acknowledgment, she went on, "Leave us, then, timorous creature!"

The Earl bowed his gratitude for her forbearance, and after a word in private with Mlle. Lutetie, which left her smiling broadly, he made his adieus.

Mademoiselle had already alerted her minions, who were displaying luscious bolts of silk, satin, velvet, and delicate crepe materials, as well as swatches of trimmings in laces, braid, and feathers. These enticements were draped over chair backs or thrown on the soft carpet like the gleaming treasure of Ali Baba for their inspection. Lady Masterson, to Pommy's dismay, was firmly resistant both to her companion's hints that the latter would be more comfortable and certainly more suitably appareled in some less fashionable emporium, and to Mademoiselle's coaxing assertion that Her Ladyship would look as lovely as a dream in that silver tissue from Lyons.

Lady Masterson, exquisite and ethereal in black silk, was smiling negation of both proposals when a pair of ladies who had been concealed in a fitting room strolled into the main salon. Recognition was instant and unfriendly. Lady Masterson acknowledged their babble of greetings and exclamations, introduced her companion as Miss Rand, a friend from Cornwall, and civilly enough asked them how they were enjoying the Season.

"Oh, above anything!" gushed the elder and less attractive of the two ladies, who had been introduced as Mrs. Rogart. "Such a pity that you have sequestered yourself from Society, dear Aurora! And are we to assume, from your presence here, that you have at last decided to rejoin the World?"

"I am assisting my young friend to select a few gowns for her sojourn in London," replied Her Ladyship repressively. But Mrs. Rogart was not to be deterred.

"Of course it is not worth *your* while buying new clothes for yourself when you never come into Society," she emphasized. "Dear Sally Jersey was just saying, a night or two ago, that she wondered what you could have done with yourself these last years. 'Probably rusticating in the country growing vegetables!' she said in her funning way! Of course everyone laughed at the idea of the once-fashionable Lady Masterson grubbing among the hay rows!"

Mrs. Rogart and her companion, Miss Petula Rogart, laughed quite heartily at this jest. "She is such a wit, dear Sally," sighed the older lady.

"Indeed?" was the rather daunting comment from Lady Masterson "When one has so *much* to say, it is inevitable one should occasionally produce something witty, I suppose." She turned away toward Pommy, and continued in quite a different tone, "My dear child, do you not like that Pomona-green crepe? I swear it will look charmingly on you!"

Mrs. Rogart would not be dismissed so lightly. She said with an assumption of regret, "It is so sad that you no longer wear colors, Lady Masterson! I can remember how prettily you looked in those violet shades you formerly affected! Black is so hard on older women, do you not agree?" and she smoothed her own cerise silk complacently. "Well, it was pleasant to meet you and your—er—protégée from the country. She will cut quite a swath among the hayfields with her green dress from Lutetie!" Cackling shrilly at her own wit, Mrs. Rogart led her daughter out of the salon.

Pommy hardly dared look at Lady Masterson. She was rather surprised to hear a firm note in the usually lachrymose voice.

"Mlle. Lutetie, please bring me that bolt of violet silk. I wish to look at it again."

Pommy espoused the material with enthusiasm. "It reflects up into your beautiful silver-gray eyes, Lady Masterson, and makes them look like wet wood violets!"

Her Ladyship glanced in a mirror as the Frenchwoman held the lustrous material near her face. "Yes, you may make me a gown from this, mademoiselle. Let us see your pattern cards, if you please!"

When the Earl came for them, his first quick glance was at Pommy. Reassured by the drugged delight on her expressive countenance, he smiled wryly at his sister-in-law.

"You look like two particularly well-satisfied kittens! Let me coax you away from your cream pot with the lure of a pretty toy for each of you."

He assisted them into his carriage, again taking the seat which placed his back to the driver, the better to survey the two ladies before him. "I must say you seem pleased with your morning's work! Have you left a single bolt of silk or a shred of lace in the shop?"

Lady Masterson's chiming laughter rang out. "Scarcely! I promise you, Austell, there was nothing further from my mind than the idea of ordering dresses for myself when I entered that ridiculously tempting place! But then Pommy and Mrs. Rogart between them made me change my intentions."

The Earl raised questioning eyebrows. "Pommy's support of my campaign I had dared to hope for, but Mrs. Rogart—?"

"Quite an unconscious ally, I can assure you!" said Her Ladyship crisply. "A more disagreeable female I have never set eyes upon!"

It was clear to Pommy that the woman's sarcasm still rankled. She said meditatively, "Mrs. Rogart put me very much in mind of a cow my uncle bought from a gypsy. It was forever lowing and waggling its enormously fat hips, and it broke the stableman's leg with a kick when he tried to milk it. 'Aaaall moo aaand no milk' was how he characterized it," Pommy imitated the soft Cornish drawl.

Lady Masterson dissolved into delighted laughter at this characterization of her recent adversary. The Earl watched Pommy's piquant little face with warm approval as he joined in the healing merriment.

Lady Masterson wiped away tears of mirth with a lace scrap of handkerchief. "Pommy my love," she gurgled, "you must promise me you will never change!" Then she eyed her brother-in-law. "I am pleased Pommy has put you in such high good humor," she told him. "You are more like to groan when you see the bill Lutetie will send you!"

"I am?" The Earl glanced defensively at Pommy's darkening face. "But did I not tell you it is Lady Masterson's birthday, Pommy, and we must all celebrate with her? No quibbling, now! You would not wish to spoil my simple pleasures, I hope? It would be too shabby of you!"

Without quite understanding what she was at, Pommy found herself asking forgiveness of Lord Austell and then of Lady Masterson. Graciously accepting her apologies, the Earl produced two white velvet boxes from his well-cut coat. The larger he handed to his sister-in-law. "—Er—happy birthday, Aurora!" he said briskly.

"Inaccurate, but acceptable, Derek," she murmured, her slender white fingers busy with the fastening on the box. It opened to reveal a bracelet of tiny flexible silver links, set with diamonds and amethysts. Her Ladyship uttered a small crow of pleasure at the charming bauble, and accorded the Earl a dazzling smile. "My thanks, Derek darling! I shall wear it—" she paused, and a slightly lost look crossed her lovely face.

"You shall wear it at the *soirée* I am giving in your honor Thursday evening," he said firmly. "By that time one at least of the new gowns will be finished, and we shall have a quiet, pleasant evening listening to your favorite music and introducing Pommy to our friends." He turned to the girl before Her Ladyship could have time to rally and state objections. "What, child? Have you not yet opened your gift? This is not at all the thing, you know! Let us have a show of gratitude and interest at once, if you please!" He grinned at her. "I shall expect an appropriate quotation, also, from Augustus Mayo's grandchild."

Pommy raised tear-bright green eyes to his smiling face. No one had ever given her a present since her parents died. Her hands shook as she tried to recall an appropriate line. Then one of her favorite sonnets came into her mind. " 'The cause of this fair gift in me is

94

wanting . . .' " she whispered, and busied herself opening the small velvet box Lord Austell had given her.

"On the contrary," retorted the Earl, in a voice which had Lady Masterson's eyes flashing to his face, "How does Shakespeare go on? 'Thyself thou gav'st, thy own worth then not knowing.' Open it, Pommy."

Pommy stared down at the thread-thin silver chain from which hung a small emerald, simple yet beautifully faceted to display its green fires. Her heart in her wide green eyes, the girl looked up at the man so close to her across the carriage.

"Oh, it is lovely, Milord, but I cannot . . . I must not . . . it is too precious—"

Lady Masterson had been observing this scene with interest. Now she addressed her companion with calming good sense. "Nonsense, child! Of course you will not spoil Lord Austell's charming gesture on my—er—birthday with missish protests! Thank His Lordship nicely and let us enjoy our drive in the Park."

Confronted with this dauntingly prosaic charge, Pommy controlled her Romantic transports, thanked His Lordship nicely, and sat clutching her first grown-up present in fiercely protective fingers. A delightful half hour was spent bowling along the pleasant roads in the Park, Lady Masterson requesting that the windows be opened so that she might observe the beauties of Nature, as well as the occupants of other carriages and coaches. She even found herself bowing and smiling as she acknowledged the pleased recognition of her person from numerous old friends.

"This has been a triumphant progression for you, my dear Aurora," the Earl commented after the twentieth such encounter. "It would appear that you should show yourself more frequently to your friends and admirers."

"Well, at least I am not rusticating in a hayfield," scoffed the widow. This remark naturally aroused Lord Austell's curiosity, and nothing would do for it but that he should be told the tale behind her words. Lady Masterson commanded Pommy to tell it, which the girl did with spirit. Soon they were chuckling heartily at the girl's inspired mimicry. Their acquaintances, beholding the mirthful behavior of the trio in the Earl's carriage, greeted it with pleasure or envy, according to their natures.

As he was handing the ladies down at the door of Number Three Portman Square, Lord Austell bent toward Pommy and said, soberly but with an unmistakable twinkle in his blue eyes, "I have not yet had my quotation from the classics, little scholar. I shall not accept that self-deprecating line from Shakespeare, you know!"

"At the risk of being too obvious, shall I say I fear the Peer, even when bearing gifts?" paraphrased the girl pertly.

The Earl gave a shout of laughter. "Miss Impudence, I see you are yourself again! You shall pay for that piece of provocation, you know! You had better have a much more flattering citation ready for me by Thursday night, or I shall impose a forfeit!" Doffing his hat with panache, the Earl saw the ladies inside the door before remounting into his carriage, which promptly rolled away down the road.

Pommy sighed. It had been a wonderful, a challenging morning, and she was feeling dazed. Lady Masterson scanned the bemused little face as they started up the grand stairway to their rooms. What was Austell up to? He had never before shown any interest in débutantes! She discovered that she was most unwilling to permit this kind child to be hurt.

"You must not refine too much on what Lord Austell says, you know, my dear Pommy," she counseled. "Although he is usually quite solemn, he is very much a man of his world, after all."

"Solemn?" questioned Pommy, more for something to say than because she wanted to explore the subject. She had a sinking feeling that Her Ladyship was warning her off the Earl, and the implications of that were painful. Was Lady Masterson telling her that the Earl was beyond the touch of a country bumpkin like Pommy Rand? Or, more humiliating, was she suggesting that her own claim upon His Lordship was stronger and of longer standing than anything Pommy could put forward?

Lady Masterson was smiling gently. "I must thank you, dear child. I really do not remember when I have spent a pleasanter morning. It seems that you and Derek have committed me, between you, to an evening of music. I must admit I am looking forward to it. It will be delightful, I promise you, for Derek does all things well. I wonder whom he will invite?"

"Not Mrs. Rogart and her offspring, I trust!" quipped Pommy, making a mock-horrified grimace.

Lady Masterson's laugh chimed out. "Oh, Pommy, you do me nothing but good! I am so pleased that Derek found you for me! He has been at me forever to engage a youthful companion, hoping it would bring me out of the megrims."

"And has it?" asked Pommy, smiling.

"You know it has, dear child! I feel like a new woman already, and when that violet silk arrives, I shall look like one!"

"And confusion to Mrs. Rogart!" pledged Pommy. Both women chuckled.

"Now we must retire to our rooms to rest until it is time to dress for dinner. I have decided to come down for it again this evening, thanks to you, child."

"Have you everything you wish, Lady Masterson?" asked Pommy, remembering her duties as companion.

"Yes, thank you. Gordon cossets me to death," answered her employer with a deprecating smile. She vanished into her exquisitely feminine suite.

Sighing, Pommy was just turning away to seek the quiet of her own room when she became aware of Mikkle mounting the stairs and peering anxiously in her direction.

"Oh, Miss Pommy! There is a young lady most eager to speak with you. I hope you will indulge her at once. She is—ah—weeping!"

"Isabelle!" guessed Pommy, for surely no other girl knew where she was to be found. Unless, of course, Forte had given the Rands her direction? Turning, she hurried downstairs after the butler. In a moment she was entering the drawing room, where a vision of loveliness stood before the flower-filled hearth, a handkerchief clutched in one hand, and tears streaming down her flawless face. Pommy took one instant to wonder again how any female could cry without causing even the tip of her exquisite nose to develop unbecoming red patches, and the next instant she put her arms around the weeping girl and hugged her.

"Oh, Pommy!" wailed Miss Boggs. *"Disaster!* I am quite undone!"

"Then we shall simply have to do you up again," said Pommy prosaically. "You are alive, Isabelle, and I will help you with your problem. Can you tell me what the trouble is? Do sit down!" and she led the weeping girl to a love seat and settled her comfortably, offering her own large clean handkerchief as a reinforcement for Miss Boggs's soaked scrap of linen.

"Oh, Pommy," gulped the vintner's heiress, her glorious complexion not at all marred by her excess of grief, "it is Papa! He has concocted such a horrid scheme that I dare not tell you of it!"

"You are going to, however, are you not?" coaxed Pommy gently. "It would be foolish beyond permission if you left me dangling at the edge of Disaster!"

"But it is I who am dangling at the edge, as you phrase it, dear Pommy," objected Isabelle with her usual lack of imagination. "Papa is threatening me with marriage to the Earl!"

"*What?*" Pommy was betrayed into an incredulous squawk. "Do you mean our Earl? Lord *Austell?*"

"If that is his name, yes," agreed Isabelle.

"But I fear I do not—comprehend," stammered Pommy. "You have scarcely met His Lordship—I had no idea he had—had offered for you—"

Isabelle sighed. "I doubt if the Earl would recognize me if he met me in his porridge," she said glumly.

Pommy, stifling the desire to smile, was privately of the opinion that any male fortunate enough to get a glimpse of Miss Boggs's perfection would find it impossible to forget her, no matter where he subsequently met her, but she did not wish to start an argument at this crucial moment in Isabelle's explanation. Instead, she patted the other girl's hand gently and asked, "Then if the Earl has not offered—?"

"It is Papa," Isabelle stated. "He is at matchmaking again! First it was Mr. Alan Corcran, but since Papa has met the Earl, nothing less will satisfy him! It is too dreadful!"

Pommy snatched at the remnants of her poise. "But

surely it must be the Earl's prerogative to make an offer, must it not? Your father cannot—"

"My papa is capable of anything," Isabelle assured her. "He has taken it into his head that Lord Austell has—has compromised me—eloped with me from my Great-aunt Sophronia's home—spent several nights with me on the road—oh, I cannot tell you all the dreadful nonsense he has talked!" Tears swelled upon her lower eyelids, threatening to fall.

"Do not cry, Isabelle," commanded Pommy. "We must keep our wits about us, do you not see that?"

"Yes, Pommy," agreed Isabelle with deep admiration. "I knew if I could just get to you with my problem, it would be solved in a twinkling!"

"Well, perhaps not quite in a twinkling." Pommy demurred. "But surely in a few days at most, if you will be good enough to give me all the details of your papa's scheme."

"I think I shall be able to do so," answered Isabelle, frowning fiercely in her effort to remember the details Pommy had requested. "First, he talked a great deal about how obliged we must be at His Lordship's condescension in rescuing me. That was the first day. Then he questioned me as to everything which had happened from the moment I left Great-aunt Sophronia's doorway. Then he quizzed me about you, Pommy, and what relationship you bore the Earl. I said," the beautiful eyes pleaded for understanding of this invasion of her friend's privacy, "that His Lordship had told me you were his niece." Upon Pommy's nod of encouragement, she continued, "The next day Papa called me into his study and told me he had made inquiries, and that the Earl of Austell had no nieces, only a nephew, Mr. Gareth Masterson, and two distant cousins, both at their last prayers."

"I am Lady Masterson's companion," Pommy managed to say quietly. What sort of vicious scandal-broth was the vintner stirring up?

"Well, I told him what His Lordship had said, but Papa only laughed and rubbed his hands in the way he has when he has made a good bargain. It was then he told me he was going to seek an interview with the Earl, and present to him the necessity of a marriage to save his own good name and mine. So I came to you. For I do *not wish* to marry the Earl!"

"What is this?" demanded a new, very masculine voice from the doorway. Gareth strode into the room and confronted the two girls upon the love seat.

Isabelle raised her lovely pale blue eyes and took in the male magnificence standing before her. "Oh!" breathed the vintner's heiress, and blushed enchantingly.

At the same moment, Gareth was caught in a stare at the exquisite beauty before him. His anger drained away visibly, to be replaced by a look of wonder and awe.

"Who," demanded Gareth without removing his gaze from Isabelle's face, "is *this?*"

"It is Miss Isabelle Boggs," said Pommy, a little annoyed at an interruption at this moment, "and her father intends to blackmail the Earl into marrying her."

"Never," said Gareth simply. "I would rather marry her myself."

"That is all very well," snapped Pommy crossly, the task of dealing with *two* beautiful nitwits presenting itself as more than she could endure, "but Mr. Boggs does not wish a mere heir when he can get an Earl."

"Would you say 'mere'?" objected Gareth. "I have a

101

fine estate and enough money to take care of a wife—as Mama has been so frequently reminding me of late."

"I do not wish to be married to the Earl," Isabelle repeated, "but it is of little use to object, for Papa has often told me that he never takes 'no' for an answer."

"Perhaps your papa has a surprise in store," said Pommy grimly. A dozen schemes were flashing through her head; if she could only secure a few minutes' peace, she would be able to decide which one offered the best chance of succeeding. She looked at the two handsome creatures before her. It seemed they had scarcely moved in the last few minutes.

"Gareth," Pommy said clearly, "why do you not ring for tea to be brought in ten minutes? I shall take Isabelle to my room, where she can wash the tears from her face. Then I shall bring her back here to you, and we three can surely find a way out of this bumble-bath."

Although it was evident that Gareth was reluctant to let the Beauty slip from his sight even long enough to wash her perfect face, he grudgingly agreed and went to summon Mikkle and relay the order for tea. Pommy escaped thankfully with Miss Boggs, whom she set to tidying up her already flawless person while her mentor sat on the bed and ran hastily through the plans which had presented themselves to her agile imagination. She had almost settled upon one, which involved flight by night to the continent, where Isabelle would be wooed and won by a Prussian nobleman of distinguished lineage, thus satisfying Mr. Boggs and freeing the Earl from the threat of blackmail, when Isabelle said idly, "My papa is going to wait upon the Earl tomorrow, during the Musical Soirée. He is sure that with all his guests present, Lord Austell will not wish to cause a scandal."

102

Pommy had an impulse to scream at her. Instead she said coldly, "Why did you not tell me we had so little time to maneuver? I had thought of a scheme which would have suited us very well, but this does not give me time to put it into action."

"I could go back to Bath and stay with Aunt Tabitha," proposed Isabelle humbly.

"No, for I think now that your papa will proceed with his blackmail whether you are in London or Land's End," said Pommy honestly. "I must tell the Earl what threatens him. It would not be fair to let him rush blindly upon his fate. You see that, do you not?"

Betraying her father's plans to the proposed victim did not bother Isabelle. She nodded happily enough and said, shyly, "That young gentleman downstairs—is he your brother?"

Pommy, in the throes of a new invention, contented herself with a brief, "No."

"Cousin?"

"No."

"Is he—your fiancé?"

"He is the Earl's nephew and heir. His name is Gareth Masterson. His style, the Honorable," explained Pommy, accepting the fact that her self-invited guest would not leave her in peace to plot a way out of their difficulties, a way of saving the Earl, until her curiosity had been satisfied. There was only one thing to do: inform Lord Austell of the danger as soon as possible, and let him save himself. It seemed poor spirited, but Pommy was sensible enough to know when she was out of her depth.

She led Isabelle down to the drawing room where Gareth waited, standing guard over the tea tray. His gaze went at once to Isabelle. She smiled shyly at him. He took her hand and led her to the love seat, where he sat down beside her. The fact that his six-foot frame rather crowded the available accommodation did not appear to disturb either of the pair.

They gazed at one another.

Sighing, Pommy poured them each a cup of tea and left them. It was more important to send a note to the Earl than to play gooseberry for a couple so besotted that they had quite forgotten she was there.

Nine

WHEN LADY MASTERSON came down to dinner she was startled yet pleased to see her son in close converse with a modishly attired and most beautiful young girl. Pommy had made sure that she herself was already dressed for dinner in her emerald silk, and was chaperoning the pair, so that Her Ladyship might not be disturbed by any flouting of *les convenances*. Gareth sprang up as his mother entered; Pommy was glad to observe that he neither flustered nor bullocked, but presented Miss Isabelle Boggs to Lady Masterson with cheerful grace, informing her that he had taken the liberty of inviting Pommy's guest to dinner.

Her Ladyship graciously seconded the invitation, but Miss Boggs, suddenly made aware that her visit had lasted quite two hours, said very prettily that she must depart at once. In spite of warm entreaties to change her mind, Isabelle remained quietly adamant.

She took her leave with all the correct civilities, and Pommy was inclined to credit Mr. Boggs with having secured the services of an excellent governess for his ewe lamb.

While Gareth was seeing the guest out to her waiting carriage, Lady Masterson fixed Pommy with an inquiring eye. "What a *very* beautiful young woman," she began.

Pommy smiled. "She is the pretty widgeon I told you of, who fell in front of our carriage." She was sure Her Ladyship had immediately recognized the girl from Pommy's description. There could surely not, even in London at the height of the Season, be two girls as ravishingly lovely as Isabelle! "A Nonesuch, is she not?"

"Quite the most beautiful creature I have ever seen," agreed Gareth's mother with commendable modesty, "and pretty behaved, as well."

There could be little doubt that Lady Masterson had also recalled the information that Mr. Boggs was as rich as Croesus, but such considerations would weigh lightly with one of Her Ladyship's wealth and lineage. What might interest her, thought Pommy, noting the speculative gleam in the beautiful silver eyes, was that this flawless-looking heiress was obviously as biddable as she was beautiful, and might serve to anchor Gareth in London. Lady Masterson smiled gently and prepared to go in to dinner with great contentment.

To her satisfaction, Gareth announced that he had thought of an excellent scheme, if his mama approved? Being urged to reveal the nature of this scheme, he said he had had the notion of procuring tickets for the theater for his mother, Pommy, and of course, their new friend Miss Isabelle ... perhaps a quiet little dinner beforehand, at a place Uncle Derek had spoken

106

of . . . if his mama thought it would not bore everyone to tears—? He looked at Lady Masterson with his heart in his beautiful eyes.

No lady, least of all his mother, could resist such an appeal. Her Ladyship said she thought it a capital plan, and she was sure they would all enjoy it very much indeed. Since it was the first time her son had ever volunteered to go on the Town, even in so circumspect a fashion, Lady Masterson positively beamed upon him. And upon Pommy, for she correctly attributed his new interest in social activities to the introduction into her household of the Earl's protégée.

Pommy said all that was proper to encourage the scheme, and no one would have known, from watching her smiling little face, that the devious brain behind it was hard at work planning not only how to apprise the Earl of his danger, but also how to assist him actively in combating it.

In the event, it was almost noon the next day before she was able to get away to deliver her warning. First, the new dresses arrived for Her Ladyship and Her Ladyship's companion from Mlle. Lutetie. These had to be tried on, criticized, admired, and finally hung up in the armoires of the two ladies. Then there was a nuncheon to be got through, for Lady Masterson, bustling and pleased with her new interests, was eager to talk to Pommy about the heartening change in Gareth's attitude. Pommy could see that her need for him was not obsessive; she did not wish to possess all his time and attention, merely to be assured that he would remain near her.

When Lady Masterson could at length be persuaded to lie down upon her bed for a rest to prepare her for the night's festivities at the Musical Soirée, Pommy escaped thankfully. She did not feel it proper in her to request the use of one of her hostess's vehicles, so she merely put on her bonnet, one of the new walking dresses which she could not resist, and smiling gently at the surprised young footman, Chelm, went out the door and into the Square.

She had marked the presence of a stand where a hackney coach might be hired. She had still a few shillings of her savings left, for the Earl had told her pretty sharply not to look a gift horse in the mouth, and then relented enough to inform her that he would send on the bill as soon as Mlle. Lutetie presented it. There was no difficulty in securing a hackney coach, and Pommy found herself before the Earl's impressive Town house in the twinkling of hooves (as she told herself with a chuckle). She was a little abstracted as she paid and tipped her Jehu, but managed to pull herself together, mount the steps under the handsome portico, and wield the knocker. When she gave him her name, the Earl's butler received her with such flattering attention that she wondered if His Lordship, on receiving her note, had given his servant a hint of her possible arrival. Within a minute she was ushered into a noble library. From behind a massive desk Lord Austell rose to greet her with a welcoming smile.

"Pommy! This is a pleasure! May I offer you a cup of tea?"

"Thank you, no, Milord. I have just lunched with Lady Masterson."

The Earl dismissed the waiting Tupper with a nod, then helped Pommy to a comfortable chair near the window, where the light fell softly over her piquant face.

"In what way may I serve you, child?" he asked gently.

With a stern admonition to herself not to be missish, Pommy began her story. By the time she had related Mr. Boggs's scheme to levy blackmail upon the Earl, he was grinning.

"So that was the reason for your frantic little note! I was about to wait upon you to discover the whole."

"You were taking your time," retorted Pommy, not at all relishing his amusement. "I had feared my missive had not been delivered, since I heard nothing from you."

The Earl's eyes were still warm with laughter. "You must forgive me, dear Pommy, but you will recollect that I am to be your host at a Musical Soirée this evening, and I am most anxious to spare no effort to make the event a pleasant one for you and Lady Masterson."

Pommy was not placated by this flummery. "You are also to be host, however inadvertently, to Mr. Boggs. It is his plan to challenge you over his daughter's excursion with you while you are surrounded by your friends—and thus may be reckoned to be particularly vulnerable to his wretched scheme!"

"An enterprising fellow!" said the Earl. "I wonder how he plans to get past Tupper and eight stout footmen?"

"Eight?" gasped Pommy. "You maintain your state, Milord!"

"Oh, it is all put on to impress you, Pommy," teased the Earl. "As a usual thing, I have only four."

"You are laughing at me again," said Pommy. "I do not know why I do not abandon you to your doom without qualms!"

"Could you, Pommy? Leave me to my doom? I had thought you had some little kindness for me," and his smiling gaze probed her flushed countenance. "Do you, dear Pommy? Have even the least affection for me?"

Pommy's honest eyes met his. A rich blush flowed up into her face. "You must know, Milord, that I—that I—"

The Earl had stopped smiling and was regarding her intently. "It is not fair of me to challenge you thus, is it, my Pommy?" he said, in quite a different tone from the teasing one he had been using. "So. Forget all this and let us discuss our plans for my salvation—for I would wager a great deal upon the fact that you have some."

Not entirely relieved by the Earl's abrupt dismissal of their relationship, Pommy was still grateful for the removal of pressure. Gathering her powers of invention, she suggested the several plans she had already considered. She found His Lordship full of quibbles and quite unreasonable objections.

"As you say, catching a foreign princeling for Miss Boggs might require more time than we have in hand. Also there would be the language barrier—still, that might be an advantage in the case of Miss Boggs. I am sure if the foreign princeling had only to look at her, he would never become bored."

"The plan to waylay Boggs himself," continued the Earl judicially, "and incarcerate him in some out-of-the-way spot, would have serious repercussions, I fear. We could not keep him *incommunicado* forever, could we? When he was finally restored to freedom, he would be sure to take umbrage at our attentions. On the other hand, the scheme for me to absent myself from London for six months on a Grand Tour has much to recommend it. Boggs could hardly blackmail me if I played least-in-sight. Still, I might get lonely. Had you envisioned a companion for me during my six months exile, Pommy?"

Pommy set her teeth. "Are you teasing me again?"

The Earl laughed. "The *simplest* way out of the

difficulty—though I know that *that* would never appeal to you, child—is for Miss Isabelle to become engaged to someone else. Did you not say she is, in fact, already publicly plighted to Alan Corcran?"

"It would humiliate her to wed him after the cruel thing he said," protested Pommy. "Besides, I have the impression Mr. Boggs would not allow a little thing like an engagement to stand in the way of making his daughter your Countess!"

"And you believe I will have nothing to say about that?" asked the Earl. "You do not know me well enough."

"Of course you could *stop* it," said Pommy. "Could you also stop the gossip he is determined to raise? And do not tell me, in that odious, toplofty manner, that you would simply ignore it, because I do know you well enough to understand how much you would hate it!"

"*Touché,*" admitted the Earl. "Then, if we cannot get the Fair Isabelle married off in time to save me, what do you say to getting *me* leg shackled?"

Pommy heard this astounding question with shocked surprise. He wasn't smiling. Instead he was watching her closely. After a moment she said in a small voice she hardly recognized as her own, "To—to Lady Masterson?"

"Of course not, widgeon! She was my brother's wife. I like her, but her endless indulgence in Moods would drive me to Bedlam! By the way, I have you to thank for rousing her out of a melancholy so prolonged I feared she had sunk in it forever!"

Pommy would not be diverted from the question. "Then to whom?"

The Earl regarded her with an odd little smile. "To you?"

Pommy opened her mouth to utter a withering diatribe against persons who treated serious matters with flippancy—and then paused. She must not take for granted that he was serious, since it had already occurred to her that, for a man who was forever teasing her about being a Romantic, the Earl had a frivolous streak—what Uncle Charles would undoubtedly have called an odd kick in his gallop. It was likely he was funning her again. She scrutinized his expression carefully. There was no trace of mockery in it. Then why this incredible suggestion? She tried to marshal her thoughts. After a moment she decided she had the answer.

"I see! That way you'd be safe. I would never hold you to it, of course, and when Isabelle was safely wedded to someone else, you could announce a change of—" she faltered—"a change of heart." She managed to get the final phrase out bravely enough.

'Would not that be a perfect chance for you to be the Blighted Heroine?" the man asked, and there was a queer twist of mockery in his face. "When we break it off, I mean. You would immediately become the most interesting young female in London, the one who had actually dismissed an Earl! I could promise to go about looking heartbroken, and having a glass too much wine upon occasion, and ruining pompous dinner parties with my sighs and gloomy looks!" He laughed harshly.

"In that case," snapped Pommy, feeling both cross and wretched at once, "it would not be myself but you—who would be Blighted, I mean. No, Milord, I find your plan unacceptable. Even in jest." (*Especially when it is in jest, dear Milord,* cried her treacherous heart.)

The Earl stood up. "On the contrary, my dear child, I think I may have hit upon the very answer to my problem. You must wear your prettiest new dress to my musical evening tonight. I shall be obviously *épris*, quite bowled over by you. That will pave the way for the announcement of our engagement—next week, shall we say?" He smiled encouragingly.

"And what about Mr. Boggs?" queried Pommy, who was not amused. Of course the Earl was joking, but his suggestion was doing uncomfortable things to her emotions.

"I shall give particular instructions to all eight of the footmen to deny Boggs *père* entrance." He took her hand in one of his big warm ones and held it for a moment. "Now, home with you, child, before Aurora rises from her couch and begins to wonder what has become of you. I shall see you tonight."

He ushered her to the door, insisted upon sending her home in his own carriage when he found she had come in a hired vehicle, and waited most courteously with her in the portico until his carriage could be brought around. During the wait he chatted pleasantly of many things, none of them subjects in which Miss Rand had the slightest interest. Just as he was handing her into his luxurious coach, she turned for a final objection.

"My Lord! This is insanity! Lady Masterson—your friends—!"

"Hush, child," he said maddeningly. "Trust me. You shall be a Heroine yet!" And then, shocking her out of further speech, he bent and placed a firm, very sweet kiss upon her mutinous lips. Then he stepped back and bowed gallantly as the carriage drew away.

Pommy was crying by this time, and thus did not see her Aunt Henga, Cousin Ceci, and Cousin Lydia staring at her from across the road. They had been driving down the fashionable street in an unfashionable hired landaulet with the top down, ostensibly to get the air,

113

but actually because they wanted to get a look at the Town house of the Earl of Austell. Ceci's sharp eyes were the first to spot her cousin talking to the same modishly dressed gentleman with whom she had fled from Highcliff. Ceci at once called her mother's attention to the sight. Mrs. Rand ordered their driver to halt. The three women watched the long and amicable discussion between the man and Pommy. Just as he was handing her into the elegant carriage which had pulled up beside them, the man bent and kissed Pommy. On the *lips!* In broad daylight! In the open street!

When the carriage had drawn away, and the Earl had gone back into his house, the three women drew a long breath.

"Well!" said Mrs. Rand. "I think I know what to make of *that!"*

"What, Mama?" asked Lydia.

Ceci, who prided herself on having already acquired some town bronze, said pertly, "Mama is distressed to think we have caught our cousin leaving a gentleman's home where she had been—ah—visiting without a chaperone."

"If *that* were all!" intoned Mrs. Rand in lugubrious tones.

"Did you see the dress he has bought her? It is smarter far than anything you have, Ceci," taunted Lydia, who had had to watch her older sister being decked out in all the prettier of the new gowns their papa had reluctantly put up for.

"I have no doubt he has bought her a number of outfits which I should be sorry to see either of my daughters decked out in," said Mama, primly. The girls were not impressed, for both of them had recognized the style and suitability of the garment Pommy was sporting.

114

"What are we to do about it?" prodded Ceci, jealously.

"I shall tell your father," announced Mrs. Rand, very much on her high ropes. "Perhaps your uncle George and he will handle the matter. It is something which should not come in the way of gently bred females."

With this Olympian pronouncement they had to be content.

Ten

BY THE TIME Pommy reached Portman Square, she had managed to control her emotions and dry her tears. She went at once to seek out Lady Masterson, and found her just rising from her *chaise longue* to dress for dinner, attended by the faithful Gordon. Pommy had not meant to burden her kind employer with the problem, but upon sober reflection she saw that the Lady Masterson would have to know of the threat which hung over the Musical Soirée and Her Ladyship's brother-in-law. Knocking softly, then, she entered the bedroom, and after returning Milady's pleasant greeting, said soberly, "I have something to tell Your Ladyship which I fear will not be comfortable hearing. Perhaps Gordon might bring you a glass of sherry?"

With a quick glance at her mistress, the dresser disappeared quietly upon her errand. Lady Masterson, her eyes bright with concern, said, "Do take off your bonnet and gloves, child, and sit down here near me! Is it something to do with your family?"

"No, ma'am. It has to do with Lord Austell and the father of that beautiful girl who was here yesterday. You remember I told you of our helping her when her servants abandoned her on the road, and how courteously Lord Austell behaved to her, as though she were a member of his own family?" Pommy's eyes were bright with indignation. "It now appears that Mr. Boggs has planned something so wicked you will not credit it!"

Being a great deal wiser in the ways of the world than her companion, Lady Masterson had already conceived a very good idea of what Mr. Boggs was threatening. She sighed with pleasure. Pure burlesque, and happening within her own house! Derek was right—the child was a catalyst. Her Ladyship had not had so much excitement in years. As for the child's fears for Derek, Lady Masterson had no doubt he would be quite capable of handling a dozen vintners. Nevertheless she listened carefully as the girl poured out her story, noting the flush of partisan anger on the piquant little face, and the sparkle of wrath in the green eyes. When Pommy had finished, Lady Masterson pursed her lips.

"You say you have just informed Derek of this wretched creature's intentions? That was wise of you, my dear. 'Forewarned is forearmed,' as I am sure one of your ancient Greeks or Romans must have said!"

Pommy decided she would never understand the Quality however long she mingled with them. Could they not see the nasty gossip which would ensue from such charges as Mr. Boggs was threatening? Did they not care? Lady Masterson took pity on her obvious distress.

117

"My dear child, I am confident that Derek offered you some sort of reassurance. What did he say?"

"He asked me to marry him," reported Pommy gloomily.

This was indeed a facer, even for Her Ladyship. That committed melancholic uttered a sharp and rather unladylike bark of laughter, which made Pommy wonder if all the members of Austell's family were incurably given to Levity.

Her Ladyship got her risibilities under control and said, with a convincing show of concern, "That is indeed one way of dealing with Mr. Boggs's encroaching behavior."

"Rather drastic, do you not think?" asked Pommy bitterly. "Like burning the barn to frighten away a stinkbug."

"An interesting bucolic comparison," replied Aurora, biting her lips to keep from breaking into peals of laughter.

But Pommy could not miss seeing the amusement sparkling in her employer's eyes. "Do you think he was funning me?" she asked in some confusion.

"Oh, no!" gasped Her Ladyship, "from what I know of Derek, he would not—er—fun about such a serious matter. He is not, I am convinced, in the habit of going about London proposing to young ladies in jest." She shook her head, still smiling broadly. "Too dangerous, you see," she explained. "Some of them might take him up on it."

Pommy stiffened. "I cannot quite see why Lord Austell and yourself view this matter as a jest, Lady Masterson," she said. "I had thought the situation might be, at the least, extremely unpleasant for His Lordship, but if he is to make a joke of it—"

At once Lady Masterson sobered. "But child, how is

118

it a jest for man to offer for you? Quite a compliment, one would think, from such a high stickler as Lord Austell!"

"But it was surely the merest badinage!" wailed Pommy.

"He told you that?"

"No, but *surely*—"

"Then he meant it. You are a very fortunate young woman, my dear Pommy. Derek has long been the despair of the matchmaking mamas."

At this moment, Gordon reentered the bedroom, bearing a tray on which reposed a Waterford decanter and two exquisite glasses. Her mistress beamed satisfaction. "As ever, Gordon, you are awake upon all suits—as Gareth would say," she added hastily, encountering a minatory look from her dresser at this use of cant. "You must pour a glass for Miss Pommy, and offer her your congratulations upon her engagement to the Earl of Austell."

Pommy waited, cringing, for the look of disapproval—or worse, scorn—which would follow Her Ladyship's announcement. Instead, a pleased smile appeared upon the Dragon's countenance, and she said, in a cordial voice, "I wish you happy, Miss Pommy, I'm sure!" As she offered the filled glasses, she continued, with a sly smile, "Of course it was plain to see which way the wind was blowing when His Lordship brought Miss Pommy to stay with Your Ladyship."

Ignoring Pommy's astounded look, the two older ladies smiled at one another. Then, since the girl merely shook her head in dazed rejection of the sherry, Lady Masterson told Gordon to drink it in a toast to Miss Melpomene Rand.

Eleven

IN A MUCH LESS fashionable section of London a council of war was in session at this moment. Mrs. Henga Rand had instructed her hired coachman to return to the rented house as quickly as possible, and once there, had emptied her budget to Squire Rand, ending with the angry demand to know what he intended to do about the scandalous goings-on of his niece—thank God, not a member of his wife's family, who had been noted for their circumspect behavior throughout two counties.

"For it is *your* name she is besmirching all over Town, Charles," she concluded sharply.

While wife and daughters hung avidly upon his answer, Squire Rand pursed his lips in and out as was his wont when mulling over an important decision. At length he nodded.

"You are sure it was the same man who came to pick her up at Highcliff Manor?"

Three female voices simultaneously assured him that it was.

"Makes it demmed awkward," ruminated the squire.

"What?" shrieked his wife.

"Fellow's an Earl, y'know. Usual rules don't apply. Can you see me offering to horsewhip him? Call him out?" asked the squire dubiously.

"Pommy isn't an Earl," Ceci pointed out. It would be too much if the despised cousin were to receive the attentions of an Earl, however clandestinely, while she herself had to make do with no better than a Baronet—and he vastly toplofty and spoiled, and possessed of a discouraging mama besides.

"The case is that I ain't in any hurry to break squares with a member of the Peerage," said the squire petulantly. "Why can't you act as if you'd never seen her? You didn't make yourselves known, I collect?"

"Of course not!" snapped his wife. "I, to speak to that—that—!"

"Then I can't for the life of me see why you're so hot to have me seek her out. If I bring her here, you'll be forced to speak to her, if only to point out the error of her ways," said her disgruntled husband.

"That is different!" his wife informed him loftily, and the girls added their chorus of agreement. Their mother told them she would thank them not to presume that *they* would be on any terms of easy conversation with one who was no better than a Fallen Woman. She added that she would know how to deal with such a female as Pommy had shown herself to be. "It is the fault of all those books," she said scornfully. "I have often warned you that no good would come of letting her waste time *reading!"*

But no measures, defensive or punitive, could be taken until the girl was back under their control. After an acrimonious discussion, it was finally agreed that the squire's brother, Colonel George Rand of the Seventh Hussars, be given the task of calling upon Lord Austell and demanding the return of his niece.

"For it is certain," claimed Mrs. Rand, "that the Earl will not have the brass to deny a member of the girl's family! And your brother, as I have often said, is a stiff-rumped military man, toplofty enough to beard even a Duke in his den! I am sure he has never put himself out to be conciliating to *me!* In fact, if I recall correctly, he had always a soft spot for Melpomene. And now we see what has come of it!"

Squire Rand did not quite comprehend how his brother George's rather tepid affection for the child Pommy could be blamed for the mull she had gotten herself into, but he forbore to correct his wife, since her proposal accorded very well with his own wishes in the matter. For one thing, he had absolutely no desire to come to points with an Earl, and was very willing to let his brother take the risks. Had he not been mentioned in dispatches by General Whitelock from South America? Let him prove his courage at home for a change! Even stronger, however, was his feeling that George had let him down badly by selling up his patrimony as soon as their father died, thus removing a large portion of land and revenue from the new squire's estate. It was understandable that he wished to purchase his commission, but was it necessary to dispose of the whole of his inheritance to do so? The memory of certain harsh comments made by George upon his older brother's inability to make a profit out of their ancestral acres still rankled. How could any man make a profit out of lands so depleted by their father's poor management? The squire decided it was no more than just that George should have to do battle with the Earl, since he was, after all, the soldier in the family.

A footman was sent round to Colonel George Rand's apartments, with an urgent request for an immediate parley. Then the squire sought out his wife and advised her that she had better make sure the dinner was better than passable, for it was well known to all of them that George was a sharp and outspoken critic of a poorly chosen or prepared meal.

In the event, Mrs. Rand and her cook were able to come up with a meal which, though it won no encomiums from the colonel, did not draw his fire, either. Further mellowing their guest with a decanter of the finest port in the cellar, the squire then related the story of Pommy's disgrace, and challenged his brother to confront his niece's seducer and bring her home.

Somewhat to the squire's surprise, the colonel rose at once from the table and asked if his brother had gotten the Earl's direction. It developed that he regarded the threat to the family name even more strongly than Mrs. Rand did, and was ready to charge to the attack that very evening. Upon hearing this, the squire hastily adjourned to the drawing room, where his wife did not fail him. She was able to supply the street and number of the elegant residence on whose doorstep her infamous niece had been observed consorting with the dissolute nobleman. Beyond telling her to guard her tongue in front of their daughters, her husband had little more to say to her, but returned to the hall where the colonel was already donning his hat and short cape.

"You might as well bring the chit back here when you get her," he offered glumly enough.

The colonel gave him a searing look but did not enlarge upon that silent comment. He had come to his brother's house in his own curricle, with a sergeant up beside him. Squire Rand, enviously watching the smart equipage tool off down the road, had no need to wonder where the money for the natty turnout had come from.

Colonel Rand's sergeant knew his London, and was able to direct the officer to the Earl's Town house within a very short range of time. It was as well for the colonel that he was so quick, for the Earl's house was blazing with lights, and His Lordship's servants had rolled a red carpet quite across the flagstones and into the street. The colonel was of two minds whether to burst in upon the Earl when he was expecting guests, but his feeling for his little niece was stronger than his brother had given him credit for. He squared his shoulders and marched smartly up the steps under the imposing portico to the front door, upon which he rapped sharply with the bronze knocker. He had no difficulty in intimidating the footman who opened it, and at once demanded to see the Earl.

'His Lordship is preparing to receive guests," said the footman apologetically.

"He had better receive me first, if he knows what's good for him," stated the colonel, carrying the battle to the enemy in rousing style. "I am Colonel Rand."

The footman admitted defeat and called upon the butler to take care of a matter far beyond his touch. Tupper was not long in taking Colonel Rand's measure and evaluating his temper, and ushered him quickly into Milord's book room, where he served him with a small glass of fine brandy to sweeten the wait. This the officer refused with every evidence of revulsion. It was not long, however, before the Earl, looking arrogant and dangerous, strolled into the library.

"You—ah—demanded to see me, sir?"

"If you are the Earl of Austell, I did," said the colonel. "Your name is Rand?"

"Colonel George Rand, Seventh Hussars," said the officer, drawing himself up to his not inconsiderable height.

"You have come about Miss Melpomene, then." The Earl took the wind from his sails, and then pursued his advantage by saying crisply, "My sister and I wondered when some member of Miss Rand's family would demonstrate enough concern to inquire after her health and welfare."

The colonel began to suspect that his stupid brother and the latter's even more stupid wife had sent him on a wild-goose chase. Still, there was a good deal here that he did not understand, and the gallant colonel was not one to turn tail at the first rebuff. He replied stiffly, "I was not informed until this evening that my niece had left her home under your—ah—protection, nor that she was—ah—a member of your household, Milord."

"She is not." The Earl sensibly ignored the first charge, where he was vulnerable, and arrogantly denied the second, where he was on firm ground.

"Where is she, then?"

"She is residing in Portman Square with Lady Masterson, my brother's widow."

This piece of intelligence knocked the colonel back on his heels, but he rattled in again quickly. "And what is my niece doing in such an elegant establishment? Are you telling me she is a maidservant there? Do not seek to gull me, sir! It will not wash! I was informed that she was seen—ah—loitering on your doorstep today, wearing a most expensive and fashionable costume and behaving—ah—indiscreetly!"

"I wonder who can be your intelligencer, Colonel?" The Earl's contempt was plain. "Miss Rand, who has been most callously treated by those whose duty it should have been to protect and nurture a defenseless orphan in their care, was thrown out of your brother's house. Fortunately, my sister-in-law was in need of a cheerful, well-educated and well-bred companion, and offered Miss Rand the position. Since the child preferred that offer to wandering around in a storm, she accepted."

Damn Charles and that archwife of his! thought the soldier. Although his cheeks were suffused with dark color, and his voice grew louder as he began to fear his position was untenable, he stuck to his guns, and demanded, "How is it, Milord, that you are so well informed of all the details of Pommy's plight?"

The Earl considered his purpling face with sardonic understanding. "I was at Highcliff Manor when she was thrown out," he said quietly.

"Then you brought her up to London with you in your carriage?" snapped the colonel suspiciously, but his heart was not in it.

"After securing for Miss Rand a female companion to act as chaperone," Lord Austell said, carrying the matter off with a high hand.

Colonel Rand knew when the battle was lost. He retreated gallantly, firing one defiant parting shot. "I shall naturally have to assure myself that my niece is safe and well. Where is she?"

"Naturally," agreed the Earl, magnanimous in victory. "She is at Number Three Portman Square. If you drive there at once, you may see her before she goes out for the evening. She is to accompany Lady Masterson to a Musical Soirée."

The colonel drew himself up and made his adieux like a gentleman and a soldier. The Earl saw him to the door with a rather malicious courtesy. Returning to his curricle, Rand gave his invaluable sergeant Lady Masterson's address and sank back on the seat, seething with embarrassment and anger. He spent the time it took to reach Portman Square in thoroughly damning his brother for a totty-headed knock-in-the-cradle who deserved the shrew he'd married.

When he got down in front of Her Ladyship's mansion, he was secretly impressed by the quality of his niece's new associates. Companion she might well be—for he remembered her as a bright, open, charming little miss, well suited to be an attendant upon a lady—but she was dwelling in a finer house than any his family had ever had, and if her clothing was as handsome as Charles had described, she was being paid a much larger salary than most companions ever hoped to earn. Becoming suspicious again, he demanded entrance to Her Ladyship's residence with a stout assault upon the knocker. By God! he'd see the child and make sure there was nothing havey-cavey going on!

Thus Mikkle, answering the thunderous pounding upon the front door, was confronted by an angry officer in full regimentals who demanded to see his niece, Miss Pommy Rand, without argument or delay.

Mikkle had far less courage than Tupper, and ushered the intimidating soldier directly in to the dining room where Her Ladyship, Pommy and Gareth were just finishing their meal. Gareth rose to confront the invader, but the soldier was suddenly frozen in the doorway, his staring eyes fastened upon the face of the Lady Masterson, exquisitely beautiful in the light of a hundred candles.

He saw a lovely woman whose fabulous silver-gray eyes gleamed between long dark lashes, whose silver-gilt hair framed the delicacy of a mature, beautiful face of such mournful sweetness that it quite won his heart. Gradually his face whitened beneath its tan. Colonel George Rand of the Seventh Hussars had surrendered, horse, foot, and sabres, to the one foe he had never expected to confront: Eros.

Lady Masterson herself was not unmoved. The tempestuous entrance of this man, incredibly dashing in his regimentals, was having a strange effect upon her breathing. She wondered if the evening had not become suddenly warmer. She looked again. He was not as handsome as the Earl, and certainly not a Nonesuch like Gareth. In fact, severe critics might call him stone faced. His hard brown eyes looked steadily out from a weather-beaten face, topped by sandy brown hair, brushed with white at the temples. His mouth was firmly set above an aggressively outthrust jaw. Aurora, experiencing an unaccustomed weakness, chided herself for behaving like a green girl at sight of a handsome uniform.

Gareth was addressing the stranger. "What can I do for you, sir? Perhaps we should leave the ladies to finish their dinner while you state your business to me—in the hall."

"My apologies," said the soldier, his bemused gaze still fixed upon Lady Masterson. "I am Colonel Rand, Seventh Hussars, and I am seeking news of my niece, Melpomene Rand—"

"Uncle George?" came a girl's voice, hesitant, unbelieving.

The soldier tore his gaze from the vision of loveliness and searched the room. A young woman, modishly dressed, had risen and was coming around the table toward him.

"You are—Pommy?" he asked, and then, meeting the direct glance of huge green eyes, his face broke into a smile which Aurora privately thought transformed his harsh visage. He opened his arms and welcomed his niece into them.

With a little gasp, Pommy ran into his embrace. He was the only member of the Rand family, outside of her father, who had ever made an affectionate gesture toward her. And she had seen him so seldom that she had been hard put to recognize him at first. After a moment, uncle and niece drew apart and looked at one another appraisingly.

"I should not have known you but for those pretty eyes," said the colonel. "You were nine, I believe, the last time I saw you." He smiled at her fondly. "You have grown into a fine young woman."

Noting how Pommy flowered under her uncle's praise, Lady Masterson mentally applauded his speech. For all he was such an impressive, even formidable figure, the soldier had warmth and compassion. Her Ladyship rose and came to stand beside the suddenly shy pair.

"Let us go to the drawing room," she suggested gently. "Gareth, instruct Mikkle to serve coffee there. And liqueurs for you gentlemen." She looked up, smiling, at the colonel, who at once offered her his arm. When she had placed her fingers lightly upon it, she directed him out into the hall and then to the drawing room, while Gareth and Pommy, whispering, brought up the rear. But alas, the harmony which seemed to be developing among the four was soon shattered. It all began with an innocuous question from Pommy to her uncle.

"How did you know where to find me, Uncle George?"

Colonel Rand frowned. "Your Aunt Henga had seen you talking to a man on the street outside his home, and took the number. The family were anxious that I—make sure of your—ah—safety. . . ."

There was an awkward silence. Gareth looked at his mother, who was frowning at the colonel. Only Pommy voiced the general unease.

"Aunt Henga! I might have guessed! So she said something horrid enough to send you here with that thunderous face—"

"But this is Mama's home, not the Earl's—" began Gareth.

Colonel Rand explained a trifle woodenly, squaring his shoulders and facing Lady Masterson. How does a man tell a beautiful woman that he had suspected her brother of being a libertine? "I called upon the Earl. He gave me this address."

All might yet have been saved if Gareth's evil genius had not prompted him to try for a joke to relieve the tension even he could feel. "How did my high-in-the-instep uncle enjoy being taken for a rake?"

There was an icy silence. Lady Masterson's glance, suddenly frigid, swept in challenge to the colonel's face. Pommy gasped, blushed, and then became pale as she took in her employer's rage.

"Ma'am," the officer, forehead bedewed, strove to mend his fences, "My Lady, His Lordship was generous enough to set me right—that is, he explained the situation. . . ."

"Indeed?" said Lady Masterson. "May I know what situation needed to be explained? I had thought my brother's name—and my own, since I am Miss Rand's employer—would have been sufficient warranty for any but the most ignorant and ill disposed—"

Setting his jaw, the colonel faced her with courage. "My Lady, I had my brother's word that Melpomene was—had placed herself in an equivocal situation."

"Ah! Your brother," repeated Her Ladyship with a smile like vitriol. "He is the one who allowed his niece to be thrown out into the storm, is he not? And his intelligencer, was, no doubt, his wife?"

"I believe so," gritted the colonel.

"You military men should always be sure your—ah—spies are completely reliable, should you not?"

Pommy could not believe that this tigress, fighting tooth and claw to avenge the slight on her brother-in-law, was the charming, lachrymose, and elegant lady who had so graciously befriended her.

Colonel Rand had had enough. Too much. Immediately after meeting the most glorious female he had ever encountered, he had been placed in a position which invited her utmost scorn. And none of it his own fault! he thought bitterly. If it were not for Pommy, so pale and unhappy at the dressing-down he was getting, he would have stalked from the accursed mansion and never thought again of its mistress! But for Pommy's sake—

"I—deeply regret that, in my ignorance, I have offended Your Ladyship," he said stiffly. "I assure you there was no intent to do more than protect a young woman of my family. I beg leave to be excused." With a formal bow to Lady Masterson, he turned to Pommy. "My dear child, it is good to see you well and happy. If you should ever care to be in touch with me, I may be reached at the Seventh Hussars. I shall reassure Charles as to your welfare, child. Good night and God bless you." With a slight bow, the colonel made an honorable retreat.

"Tactless of me," said Gareth remorsefully. "I was only trying to be funny. He seemed such a decent chap—"

"Oh, get ready to take us to the *soirée*," said his mother, so crossly that Gareth and Pommy exchanged anxious glances as they hastened to obey.

Twelve

THE GUESTS were already arriving for the Musical Soirée when Lady Masterson's fashionable carriage deposited Her Ladyship, Pommy, and Gareth at the Earl's door. Pommy was most impressed by the elegance of Milord's mansion when it was lighted for a gala evening. She and Gareth followed a still tight-lipped Lady Masterson into the great central hallway. Tupper swept toward them majestically past a double row of footmen—eight of them, Pommy counted—in their velvet coats and powdered wigs. He led them to the ballroom whence, over the babble of conversation, could be heard the distinctly unmelodious squawks, screeches, and twangings of an orchestra in process of tuining up. Gareth peaked his eyebrows in a glance of pure horror at Pommy, who found herself compelled to smother a chuckle. Then they were entering the great ballroom.

The Earl, magnificent in dark crimson and gold, came forward to kiss Lady Masterson's hand and greet Pommy and Gareth with a smile which Pommy privately thought irresistible. He took her hand, but did not kiss it. Then, offering his arm to his sister-in-law, he led her party to seats near the front of the huge room. Pommy followed Lady Masterson and found herself on the aisle, with Gareth directly behind her in the next row. To their left, French doors opened onto a formal garden, where fairy lights gleamed among the leaves of several trees. Thankful for the promise of cool, fresh air, Pommy looked around her.

Upon a slightly raised dais, banked by greenery and baskets of flowers, the members of the orchestra fluttered and rustled like a flock of blackbirds settling into an enormous nest. Within a few moments, as though they had been waiting for Lady Masterson's arrival, the orchestra began its first number. For all their discordant preliminaries, their music swelled, sweetly sonorous, into the room.

"Bach," whispered Lady Masterson. "Do you know it?"

"No. But I like it," Pommy whispered back, hoping her employer would not wish to converse throughout the program. She was aware of other whispered conversations going on all around her, and began to feel a little annoyance on behalf of the musicians who were working with such concentration to present the composition. Before she realized what was happening, Pommy had lost herself in the elegant, convoluted labyrinth of the music.

She was recalled, almost with a sense of shock, by the light pressure of her employer's hand upon her arm. Turning bemused eyes, she saw a sympathetic smile upon Lady Masterson's face.

134

"You enjoyed that, did you not?" Her Ladyship's voice was barely audible above the sudden chattering which signaled the conclusion of the composition. "Now we shall have refreshments."

Pommy sighed as they rose from their chairs. "It was like wandering through a garden maze! On every side, green leaves, and beneath one's feet a firm footing, leading one to the heart of the labyrinth . . . where a bird sang . . . promising fulfillment, if only I would persevere. I felt myself on the brink of discovering the secret center of the maze, but always paths led me away from my heart's desire—"

"Pommy!" the Earl's voice sounded at her shoulder with an urgent note she had not heard in it before. She turned quickly.

Lady Masterson intervened with a light laugh. "Yes, Derek, the child is a poet, but I must speak to you privately at once. There has been a new and quite unpleasant development."

The Earl's voice changed as he turned to speak to his nephew. "Gareth, I leave Miss Rand to your care. See that she has some ratafia and biscuits. The concert will resume in half an hour."

Then he was ushering his sister-in-law from the ballroom, his hand possessively under her elbow, or so it seemed to Pommy. The silver-gilt hair brushed against the Earl's shoulder as they moved away. Pommy followed their progress as long as she could distinguish the Earl's dark head above the crowd. Then she turned and was embarrassed to see that Gareth was watching her with sympathetic eyes.

"Sure you want the ratafia?" he asked. "It's pretty sickly stuff, but you females seem to enjoy it."

"Yes, thank you," answered Pommy, more to get rid

135

of his pitying glance than from any thirst for the disparaged offering. "What is it?"

Gareth grinned. "It's a liqueur flavored with almonds and peach pits and the like—very sweet."

"I'd like to try it."

"Right. We'll find you a place to sit and I'll bring it to you. Can't let you do battle with that mob!" and he indicated the fashionable throng crowding to get through the doors to the dining room, where tables of refreshments were set up.

"I'd like very much to go out under the trees," said Pommy wistfully. She was finding her first introduction to the *Beau Monde* overpowering. "It seems so pleasant out there—and so quiet!"

Gareth, glancing distastefully at the crowd of guests, nodded agreement. "Find yourself a comfortable spot. I'll be out as soon as possible."

Thankfully Pommy escaped into the peace of the gardens. She was too restless to wish to be seated, partly, she admitted to herself, because of the sight of that shining dark head bent so closely above the silver-gilt one in an attitude of attentive protection. If only someone would show that much concern for herself! Pommy had seldom felt so lonely, so much the Blighted Heroine, even in the days when Aunt Henga had been at her most unpleasant. She strolled miserably through the Earl's charming plantings on a path of clean white gravel, neatly raked. Once, from a vine-covered arbor, she heard soft laughter and a man's coaxing voice. It was apparent that some at least of the Earl's guests were making harmony of their own. With a sharp pang of envy, Pommy walked away quickly, so quickly that she bumped into a solid figure at the bend of the path.

Instantly a pair of arms shot out to keep her from falling, and she was pulled close to a manly chest.

136

"Oh! . . . thank you!" breathed Pommy.

"What a delightful encounter," said a youthful, mocking voice. "Are you running away from, or toward, someone?"

Pommy peered up in the dim light to observe a good-looking face wearing a saturnine grin. The elaborately casual styling of his blond hair would have told her that he was adopting the mode of the Corinthian, had she had enough *nous* to recognize it. What she did recognize was a young, dissolute-looking face, weary gray eyes, and a smile which struck her as more desperate than dashing.

"I was attempting to avoid playing gooseberry to a pair of sweethearts," she explained soberly. "You may release me now. I am quite steady on my feet, thanks to your help."

The dashing stranger gave her a searching look. "I do not know you, do I? Surely such a gorgeous creature could not have entered the scene without my being aware of it? You are new to the *Ton—*"

"It is not worth your while to play off your gallant compliments upon me, sir, for I am merely Lady Masterson's paid companion," said Pommy prosaically.

After a startled instant, the young man laughed rather harshly. "Then Lady M. must pay you a good deal more than most such wretched females usually receive, for you seem a pattern card of elegant simplicity."

"How can you tell?" asked Pommy. "It is almost too dark out here to see one's nose before one's face."

The young gallant was betrayed into a chuckle, but he persisted in his rôle. "A man can always see a lovely lady," he instructed her loftily. He continued to hold her, now quite brazenly assessing her face and figure. "Item one: a handsome gown, very ingénue but obvi-

137

ously very expensive, of some pastel color—hard to determine in this shadowy retreat. Item two: a cloud of night-black hair, most fetchingly arranged by Her Ladyship's dresser—the style is too perfect for your amateur hands to achieve. Item three—"

"Item three," warned Pommy sternly, "I shall tip you a wisty castor if you do not unhand me this instant!"

This time his laughter was a boy's, full and free, as Pommy's captor released her and stepped back a pace. "Item three: a pair of magnificently stormy eyes, which could do a man more harm than any blow from your soft little fists! And item four: a vocabulary which I'll wager you have not displayed to Lady M.!"

"My uncle's coachman was always threatening the groom in that phrase," explained Pommy. "What *is* a wisty castor? It sounds dire!"

The blond gentleman was chuckling. "The term is boxing cant. I do not believe your employer would thank me for encouraging you in its use," he said. "By the way, my name is Alan Corcran. May I know yours?"

Pommy's eyes widened. "You are Mr. Alan Corcran? But I have met your fiancée, Miss Isabelle Boggs—"

All traces of humor left Corcran's face. "You know Miss Boggs?" he asked.

"Yes. We rescued her when her coach broke down on the way to London." Pommy regarded him doubtfully. Had Destiny led her to walk in this shadowed garden, to meet Alan Corcran? It must have been a kindly Fate which had brought her to him, for he was the one person who could immediately and definitely thwart Mr. Boggs's blackmailing scheme. "I am glad now that I ran into you," she said quickly. "I must inform you that your father-in-law-to-be has conceived a most dastardly plan against Lord Austell. He is going to claim that His Lordship has compromised Isabelle's reputation—and that *he* must marry her!"

Instead of the outrage or at least alarm she had expected to see upon the face of Isabelle's intended, Pommy was shocked to observe a wide grin. "Is he, now?" breathed Alan. "A wily old trickster, our Thomas! First me and then the Earl. Well, better Masterson than me!"

Pommy glared at her new acquaintance. "How can you be so—so rag mannered! Lord Austell has interests in—another quarter, and he must not be trapped by this odious father of Isabelle!"

"Oh-ho! So that's the way the wind blows, is it?" sneered Corcran. "The little companion raising her eyes above her station?"

The words were scarcely past his sneering lips when Pommy's hand connected sharply with his cheek. "I thought Mr. Boggs was odious! I see now that you and he are evenly matched!"

Corcran's hand had gone to his slapped cheek, but rather than seeking reprisal, he was staring intently at the small, angry countenance before him. "You are not on the catch for the Earl?"

"Of course I am not, you silly creature! I have told and told you that I am Her Ladyship's companion! I am very well aware indeed of my inferior position in the social order—Ceci and Aunt Henga have seen to that most effectively!" She ended in a low, anguished tone.

"And who are Ceci and Aunt Henga? No, don't enlighten me!" he added hastily. "From the sound of your voice when you mention them, they must be the most overbearing and hidebound of females. Have they been impressing you with your lack of worth?"

Pommy caught her breath at the acute intuitiveness of the young Blade's comment. "It is only natural that my aunt should not be too happy at being encumbered with the care of a destitute niece, when she has two daughters of her own to launch into Society," she answered slowly. "Aunt Henga was kind enough to give me a home when my grandfather died, so I am showing myself less than grateful to be talking about her in such a fashion."

"It is sometimes hard to show proper gratitude," admitted Alan ruefully. "As a younger son—and a pretty unsatisfactory one at that!—I know exactly how it is to be forced to be forever offering thanks for things one would rather not have had in the first place."

Pommy, listening to the strong emotion in Alan's voice, was beginning to believe that her first, superficial judgment could easily have been at fault. To be a disregarded younger son could not be comfortable, as she had gathered from the Highcliff servants' references to her own father. Was Corcran exiled from estates he loved with all his heart, compelled to play the butterfly in the *Ton* when every feeling rebelled— to laugh when his heart was breaking? Had he perhaps even been forced to offer marriage with an heiress he could neither love nor respect? Her vivid imagination was off and running. Her great eyes dark with compassion, she placed one small hand on his arm.

"I am sorry to hear of your unhappiness, but consider, Mr. Corcran! Whether you wish to marry Isabelle or not, it is surely not your desire to see another man blackmailed into doing so?"

The Blighted Hero looked at her with lifted eyebrows. "Why should I care for Austell's dilemma? If he has compromised the girl, it is his duty to right the matter."

"But he hasn't! Compromised her, I mean. I was there all the time. He could not have been more—more—"

"Avuncular?" suggested the graceless Corcran with a grin. "So he has compromised the two of you, has he? A regular rakehell! I know which of you I'd offer for, if I were threatened with a parson's mousetrap."

"Well, you can be quite at your ease, for Isabelle doesn't wish to marry you, and I certainly don't!" huffed Pommy.

"Is that a challenge, Miss . . .? What is your name, anyway? I've given you mine most properly, but you have been reticent. Is it Cinderella, by chance?"

"It is Melpomene Rand," she said repressively, for this young man seemed very bold to one who had lived in the quiet backwater of a small Cornish village. Besides, for some reason unknown to her, she resented quite bitterly the phrase "regular rakehell" which the youth had applied to the Earl. For the first time she fully understood Lady Masterson's anger at poor Uncle George, when he had implied his own fears that his niece had fallen into the hands of an unprincipled man. And then, staring up challengingly into Alan's face, she caught a glimpse again of the rather unhappy, disappointed youth under the mask of the sophisticate. In a softer voice she continued, "It is not an unmixed joy, living in London, is it? There seems to be an almost frantic search for amusement, or advancement, and a brittle kind of relationship which do not seem to me to be at all comfortable!"

"You foolish child—" began Alan, when both of them heard a male voice calling softly, "Pommy? Where the deuce have you got to?"

Along the path came Gareth, balancing a full glass in each hand. "Oh, there you are! You'll have to toss this down quickly, you know. The concert is about to resume—worse luck!"

He had reached them by this time, and his glance

141

slid quickly over the stocky male figure so close to Pommy's. "Do I know you? Oh, it's you, Corcran." This last in no very welcoming way.

"Yes, it is I, conspiring with Miss Rand as to how we may save her employer's brother from being victimized by the rascal who dragooned me into offering for his daughter."

"Dragoon? You are referring to Pommy's uncle?" stammered Gareth, never very quick in the uptake.

Pommy smothered a reprehensible desire to laugh. At this moment, Gareth reminded her no little of Isabelle—the beautiful, anxious face, the struggle to comprehend the shift and thrust of quicker minds, the deadly absence of relieving humor. "This gentleman was—maneuvered into offering for Miss Isabelle, and neither of them really wish for the match—"

"Corcran!" growled Gareth. "You have dared to bandy about the name of that peerless lady—!"

"Do be easy, Gareth," advised Pommy wearily. "I am sure you would not wish Isabelle to marry where there was no love on either side, would you?"

"No," agreed Gareth devoutly.

"And Isabelle is my friend. It is quite permissible for Alan to discuss with me the means of saving her from the nasty machinations of her rogue of a father, is it not?"

"Yes," said Gareth, smiling for the first time since he had encountered Corcran.

"It is now become quite urgent that steps be taken, Gareth, for you yourself were present when Isabelle came to inform me that her wretched parent was trying to blackmail the Earl into offering for her, which she does not at all desire."

"She does not?" queried Gareth with great interest.

"She does not," repeated Pommy firmly. "Neither, I

142

must tell *you*, Alan, does she desire to be wedded to you—for reasons which you understand very well."

Corcran seemed torn between a conventional expression of disappointment and a gasp of heartfelt relief. He contented himself with the remark that of course any man would be desolate at losing the opportunity of a closer relationship with such an admirable lady; both gentlemen seemed to feel that he had expressed himself with correctness and sensibility; they began to adopt a much more friendly attitude toward one another. For this last, Pommy was thankful. It had appeared to her for a few charged moments that she might have to separate a pair of fighting cocks. However, the trio had hardly had time to agree to put their heads together to discover a means of outwitting Mr. Boggs when a very cold voice challenged them.

They turned like three guilty children to perceive the Earl himself standing not four feet from them and regarding them with what, even in the dim light, could be seen to be a very disapproving face.

"Is there some explanation for this—nocturnal tête-à-tête?" queried the Earl of Austell, frigidly. "No, do not try to think of one," he continued, with what Pommy felt was singular injustice. "You will please to escort Miss Rand back to the ballroom, Gareth, where the musicians are waiting to begin."

Feeling like a naughty child receiving punishment, Pommy made her way along the path a few steps ahead of Gareth. She found herself becoming more and more angry at the Earl with every step she took toward the ballroom, and when finally Gareth ushered her through the french doors and to her seat beside Lady Masterson, her color was very high indeed and her eyes were glowing green fire. It did not help at all that Lady Masterson, instead of being angry or disapproving, sent her a very shrewd look, followed by a small, knowing smile which quite infuriated Pommy.

Somehow the second half of the concert left her cold. It was impossible to forget the importance of the conference Lord Austell had interrupted. Even more difficult to dismiss from her mind was the unaccustomed coldness of his voice and manner. By the end of the performance, Pommy had convinced herself that Lord Austell, like all her relatives, was pleasant or unpleasant as the whim took him, and had no real knowledge of or regard for the feelings of one who was of lowly station and unimpressive appearance. This conviction naturally encouraged the headache which had been threatening since she left the garden, and Pommy was more than ready to agree with her employer when Lady Masterson announced that she wished to leave without partaking of further refreshments.

Her "Oh, yes, please, let us!" was in fact so woebegone that Lady Masterson glanced at her with concern, and hastened their departure. Pommy did not open her mouth during the drive home, except to murmur agreement to her employer's casual remarks about the music. Gareth said nothing at all. It was a silent trio who took their separate ways to their bedrooms in Portman Square.

Thirteen

THE FOLLOWING DAY, the massive knocker on the door of Number Three Portman Square thundered so often that Mikkle began to hope the Great Days were returning, when all the *Ton* beat a path to the doorstep of the popular Lady Masterson. First to call was the Earl, who demanded to see Miss Pommy. On being asked respectfully to wait in the drawing room, he informed Mikkle that he did not intend to wait for long, so Mikkle had better send a maid up to Miss Rand's room at once. This importunate demand was accompanied by the sour comment that most persons would already have broken their fast by this hour, which comment Mikkle ignored, convinced that His Lordship was the Victim of Love and thus could not be judged as a rational man.

As it happened, Pommy had indeed already eaten, and was sitting in her room crying and mending a rent in the new dress she had worn the previous night. On receipt of the Earl's summary command, she wiped her eyes, blew her little nose, and hurried down to the drawing room to confront Lord Austell.

After entering the room almost at a run, she halted to stare nervously up at the man who was standing with his back to the hearth, frowning at her.

"You wished to see me, Milord?" she managed to say.

That was the trouble. Derek Masterson had wanted to see Pommy Rand with an urgency which alarmed him. Although he had been a bachelor for enough years to have come to accept it as the most desirable of states, he had been constantly subjected to attack, both open and subtle, from the most beautiful débutantes in the *Beau Monde,* and their determined mamas. He had also been the recipient of lures cast out by a number of highborn ladies who had something other than matrimony on their minds. Through these traps and snares he had woven a wily path of self-preservation for so many Seasons that he had come to accept it as a fact of life that he should never wish to marry. When he had found himself making the incredible suggestion to Pommy that she marry him to save him from Boggs's machinations, the Earl was more startled than the girl who listened to the outrageous proposal. He knew he should have felt an overwhelming relief when the chit refused to take him seriously. Instead of which he found himself resentful at the complete lack of worldly wisdom she displayed in rejecting the best offer she was ever likely to receive. Of course he had been teasing her, he told himself; yet it was distinctly unflattering to get so prompt and total a repulse.

She has probably been attracted by Gareth's handsome face, he told himself gloomily, and his youth and charm, into imagining she has a *tendre* for him. But

146

this, as he analyzed it further, would not do, for he knew his Pommy's quick wits and bright mind, and could not believe that the well-meaning but knuckle-headed Gareth would win her true love.

Still, he chided himself, is not many a bright, even brilliant man ensorcelled by some empty-headed little wanton? He had seen it often enough among his own friends! Why then might not an intelligent young woman lose her heart to a slow-top? At this point he recollected Alan Corcran. Even yet he had not admitted to himself that his fury at discovering Pommy with not one but two cavaliers in his own Romantic gardens the previous night had been anything other than a sense of angry disgust that the little Heroine had so easily accepted the first overtures which came her way. And her cavaliers! The most notorious of the younger Bucks and his own nephew, beautiful but stupid. If he had realized, he told himself with searing contempt, that all the little chit wanted was a pair of male arms and lips, he himself could have—

With a feeling approaching horror, the Earl caught himself up from such dangerous imaginings. So the anger which he now proceeded to vent upon the trembling girl was, had she known it, chiefly directed against himself. When she had asked him if he wished to see her, his reply was unnecessarily violent.

"Not very much, after last night, Miss Rand! But since I am responsible for bringing you to London, and establishing you in this house, I must accept the further responsibility of seeing that you do not bring disgrace upon my family."

This shock of that attack quite drove the color from Pommy's face, revealing the dark shadows under her green eyes. For the Earl was not the only one who had had a restless night. Pommy had lain awake into the

147

small hours, trying to understand what had made Lord Austell so angry with her in the garden, and crying over lost hopes she dared not admit she had cherished.

After a minute of silence, the Earl said gruffly, "I had not meant to criticize you so sharply, child, but you must be more circumspect in your—Romantic encounters if you wish to escape the censure of the Quizzies."

Pommy held her head high. "What you observed in the garden was not a Romantic encounter, Milord. I was hot and wished to enjoy the peace and beauty of the place while Gareth—at your instructions, Your Lordship—fetched me a glass of ratafia. I was removing myself from the neighborhood of an arbor in which a couple were exchanging—ah—civilities, when I literally ran into Mr. Corcran." Recalling their own first meeting at the Climbing Man, she admitted honestly, "I seem to make a habit of running impulsively into someone's arms by mistake."

"It is not usually considered necessary to stay there, however," said the Earl grimly. She had actually been in Corcran's arms, eh? It was worse than he had thought.

"I did *not* stay there," retorted Pommy with pathetic dignity. "I discovered very soon who he was, and informed him that his fiancée's father was about to try to compromise you."

"Since we know from Isabelle that he had little stomach for the marriage, I'll wager he was delighted to hear that," said the Earl angrily. "What other details of my private affairs have you scattered about London?"

Pommy set her jaw against the remorse and shame which swept over her at this scathing denunciation. "Gareth, Alan, and I were trying to find some way to

148

circumvent Mr. Boggs's dastardly scheme when you—found us," she concluded miserably.

Although there was a measure of relief in the Earl's mind at these innocent disclosures, he found it impossible to adopt the softer tone he had begun to wish to use. The sensations he had experienced since coming upon the three in the garden last night had shaken him quite out of his bachelor complacency, and he had not yet been able to regain the facade of easy yet imperturbable detachment which was the face he was accustomed to present to his world. So now he said, rather too brusquely, "It does not do to get a reputation for disappearing into the shrubbery with your cavaliers, Pommy. If you were otherwise circumstanced, of course—" The Earl meant to refer to the fact that this darling girl was an orphan, and lacking the support and protection of a loving family. Pommy, however, who had been too shocked and hurt by Lord Austell's earlier denunciations to look for a kindly meaning in his words, immediately supposed that he was referring to her position in his sister-in-law's household.

Drawing herself up with all the dignity her trembling body would support, she said in a cold little voice, "You need not fear that I shall offend or disgrace Lady Masterson, sir! I understand what my position as her companion entails, and I shall not accompany her again to a social engagement. Indeed I would not have gone to your home last evening, except that she insisted you had included me in your invitation. I know my place, sir, and shall not step beyond it in future."

Her little face was so white that the heavy shadows under her eyes were dark stains, and her soft mouth trembled. "May I be dismissed, Milord? I have work to do."

Derek cursed himself for a clumsy, heavy-handed

fool. What had possessed him, normally an urbane and self-controlled man, to blast the child with such harshness? Before he could reply to her last speech, which revealed that she had quite mistaken his meaning, Mikkle opened the door and announced, "Mr. Alan Corcran, Milord. To see Miss Rand."

Pommy had thought her situation could not be worsened. She now perceived she had been mistaken. The Earl's face, which had seemed to soften after her last speech, now assumed a look of such fury that she quaked before it.

"You have given this fellow permission to call upon you here?"

"Indeed, Milord, I have not," cried poor Pommy.

The Earl, ignoring her, said coldly to the young sprig who, arrested by his icy glare, hesitated in the doorway, "Miss Rand was just about to attend upon Lady Masterson. You may state your business to me, sir."

"The devil I will," snapped Alan, who had had all he could stomach of stiff-rumped aristocrats. "You are neither the lady's husband nor her employer!"

The noblemen glared at one another like two large dogs in dispute over territory. Pommy, horrified at this new contretemps, said in a choked voice, "Oh, *please—!* Alan, thank you for your courtesy in answering my summons. I shall be in touch with you later. I must go to Lady Masterson now."

"You will be good enough to inform her that I am waiting to see her," instructed the Earl arrogantly.

Pommy scuttled out of the room. If she had hoped to prevent a confrontation by her lie about summoning Alan, she was far off, for the gentlemen, instead of bidding one another a civil good day, stood glaring as the door closed softly behind the girl.

150

"So she *did* send for you," began Lord Austell nastily. "She told me at first she had not."

"Well, she hadn't," retorted Alan angrily. "You've got the poor girl so frightened she doesn't know what she's saying."

"Since you are taking such an interest in the 'poor girl,' I must ask if your intentions are honorable—*this time,*" sneered the Earl.

"As a matter of fact, they are," snapped Alan, rather to his own surprise.

Looking as though he had just been tipped the settler Pommy had promised Alan, the Earl rattled back gamely, "I understood you were engaged to Miss Boggs?" he said acidly. "Or do you intend setting up a harem?"

"That will hardly be necessary," a reluctant grin was spreading over Alan's rakish countenance, "since I am given to understand that Mr. Boggs has decided that an Earl is better value for his pounds and pence than a mere second son of a Baron."

"He'll catch cold at that," said the Earl grimly.

Alan regarded the big nobleman with a grin. "I told Gareth and Pommy the old conycatcher would never gull you, but they insisted you were hooked."

"I am," confessed the Early wryly, "but not by Mr. Boggs's beautiful daughter."

Alan looked as though he would like to inquire further into the matter of His Lordship's Fair Fatality, but after a shrewd glance at the Earl's frowning countenance, he forbore. Instead he ventured, "Since I am able to assure you, sir, that my intentions are honorable, may I have your permission to call upon Miss Rand?"

The Earl, who had just moments before Seen The Light, was not surprised at his instant hostility to this callow and presumptuous proposal. "Since I am neither

151

the young lady's husband nor her employer—as you have been so quick to remind me!—I cannot dictate what she will do or whom she will receive during the hours when she is not in attendance upon Her Ladyship." He moved toward the door. "Mikkle will show you out. I must talk to Lady Masterson."

Mr. Corcran took his leave promptly, not wishing to push his luck too far. An hour later a letter was delivered to Miss Rand in her room, to which she had been gently dismissed when Lord Austell was admitted to Lady Masterson's sitting room. Scanning it with considerable difficulty—for Alan wrote a wretched scrawl—Pommy was startled to read the following:

Dear Pommy: Your employer's brotherinlaw has given me Permission to court you. As for Boggs' scheme to trap his l-ship, Austell tells me it has no chance for success, since he has already lost his Heart to Another!! With his mony and position, A. could have had any girl he chose this last ten yrs. so I must suppose his Heart is given to One who cannot or will not accept it. He was in such a frett to speke to Lady M that he as good as pushed me out of the house. Could Lady M be the Object of his affections??
I shall hope to see you as soon as you are given a free hour. Send to me when you can—only better not tonight, as I am already engaged for cards with friends.

Forever yrs to command,
Corcran.

Pommy deciphered this missive with mixed feelings. It was balm for her sore heart to know that Alan counted himself "forever hers to command"—with the exception of this evening, of course. It was enraging to be told that the Earl had given Alan permission to press his suit. What had Lord Austell to say about Pommy's marriage plans? Stirring up righteous indignation at the Earl's assumption of authority helped a little to ease the pain of knowing he cared nothing for her personally. It gave her unexpected anguish to learn that Lord Austell's affections were most likely set upon Lady Masterson—although, remembering the dark head leaning so protectively over the silver-gilt one, it was hard to deny the possibility. Yet the Earl had done so! Perhaps he was just brushing aside an encroaching servant who had no right to ask questions. Well, if it was Lady Masterson the Earl wanted, anyone who had the Earl's best interests at heart must do her possible to further the match, decided Pommy. Facing her own grief at Alan's disclosure, she was honest enough to accept that her own affections were irretrievably given to the big handsome nobleman who had entered into her fantasies so delightfully during the trip to London. With a pang she realized that actually *being* Blighted was far less amusing than imagining oneself in that position.

It remained now only to decide how best to help Lord Austell. Could it be true that Mr. Boggs would easily be persuaded to relinquish his plan to ensnare the Earl? Better to make very sure of that. Pommy considered that if Isabelle were safely wedded to anyone other than the Earl it would protect him from the vintner's schemes. Being affianced was not enough, obviously, since Mr. Boggs had callously broken off his daughter's engagement to Corcran as soon as bigger game was in sight. Pommy was smart enough to realize that she could not hope to reestablish the commitment between Isabelle and Alan—neither of them desired it. But there must be someone to whom Isabelle's superb beauty and equally superb fortune would be a lure. . . .

Help came unexpectedly, heralded by a light tapping upon Pommy's door. She opened it to discover Gareth standing in the hall, an expression of extreme anxiety upon his face.

"Do you know why Uncle Derek is closeted this age with my mother?" he asked in a conspiratorial whisper.

Pommy feared she knew only too well, but she was not one to gossip, so she returned a question. "Haven't you any idea?"

"I am afraid they are cooking up a match for me," the beautiful youth said gloomily. "They are both on at me forever to get myself into harness! Mother thinks it would anchor me here in Town. My uncle says it would make a man of me. I had hoped you might have an inkling as to the subject of their present discussion."

Pommy was struck with a formidable idea. "Do you know if they have some specific young lady in mind for you?" she asked.

"Not that I have heard," replied Gareth despondently. "I have not formed a partiality for any of the endless stream of suitable females they have been introducing me to this past Season."

"Have you no preference at all?" asked Pommy crossly. "Surely there must be some charming girl who has caught your fancy?"

A sudden light entered Gareth's eyes, making his whole face radiant. "There is one," he began. Then his face fell. "They would never let me marry her," he concluded sadly.

"Why not?" prodded Pommy.

"Because her wretched father has been trying to foist

154

the poor girl onto Uncle Derek," explained the youth, disconsolately.

"You don't—you *can't* mean Isabelle?" breathed Miss Rand, her eyes shining.

"Why can't I?" retorted Gareth crossly. "She's by far the most beautiful girl I've ever seen, and so—so conversable!" He went on, to Pommy's amazement, "I can talk to Isabelle as I never could to one of those flibbetygibbety débutantes! She listens to me, and doesn't interrupt, and I find I can express my ideas more clearly to her than to anyone—even Mother."

"Have you spoken to Isabelle?"

"About marrying me?" Gareth laughed without humor. "How can I? Mama and Uncle Derek are sure to think she is in the blackmailing scheme with her father. She would be the last person either of them would consider suitable for me." The beautiful youth sighed despondently. "My life is ruined."

That was all Pommy needed. Instantly her heart was melted, her imagination roused, and her forces recruited.

"Dear Gareth, let us find out whether Isabelle feels for you the same tender emotions you have just expressed for her!" She conveniently ignored the fact that Gareth's "tender emotions" had been limited to satisfaction at Isabelle's ability to listen to him without interrupting, and a nod of admiration toward her beauty. Her partisanship was easier because she recalled Isabelle's deep and evident *empressement* over Gareth's appearance, and her too-casual inquiries as to whether he was Pommy's brother, cousin, or fiancé. She felt a momentary qualm at betraying her employer by encouraging her son to make a questionable alliance, for it was plain Gareth was expected to marry a girl of his own order. To a high stickler such as Lady Masterson, even the wealth of a Croesus would not be sufficient to remove the taint of Trade from the vintner's daughter, while Lord Austell could scarcely be expected to accept with equanimity the possibility of being connected by his nephew's marriage with the man who was presently trying to blackmail him.

Still, what else was she to do? It was evident to the meanest intelligence that Gareth could not easily be persuaded to marry where his interest was not involved: witness his mother's unsuccessful attempts to get him shackled to any girl of the *Ton*. But he had displayed a remarkable interest in Miss Boggs, and she in him. It was also evident that Miss Boggs must be married if Lord Austell was to be saved from social disaster.

Pommy frowned with the complexity of the problem. Gareth and Isabelle between them had hardly enough sense to come in out of a rainstorm, but they had taken an instant liking to one another and would be happy and comfortable together. If Lady Masterson was too indignant to forgive them at once, they could retire to Gareth's estate and be happy, while Lord Austell consoled Lady Masterson for her loss of an escort by marrying her and giving her his right arm and the rest of his splendid body to lean upon.

Somehow the very thought of that eventuality so depressed Pommy that she had little heart for the machinations she would have to perform to bring about the desired end. She took herself sharply to task. What did it matter that her own feelings were cruelly lacerated, as long as Lord Austell was happy and safe from scandal? Swallowing a painful lump in her throat, Pommy accepted the fact that her perfidy toward her kind employer would result in her instant dismissal and ejection from this house into the hostile streets of

London. And of course she would never see Lord Austell again— But he would be happy with his Aurora. . . .

"Why," asked Gareth in bewilderment, "are you crying, Pommy? Do you have the headache?" It occurred to him that his mother frequently seemed to develop a headache when he tried to talk her into letting him visit his estate. Perhaps women's brains were too delicate to sustain a serious conversation with a man? And yet Miss Boggs had seemed most happy to converse with him. Her lovely brow had remained quite unfurrowed and she had even appeared anxious to continue their tête-à-tête! It seemed to Gareth that his Isabelle—for so, with Pommy's encouragement, he now dared to regard her—was unusually intelligent for a woman. Beautiful, kind, intelligent! A Nonpareil! He set his well-shaped mouth in a stubborn line. Headache or no headache, Pommy must carry through with the task she herself had just suggested, that of finding out whether the beautiful Miss Boggs felt for him what he now realized he felt for her: to wit, Love.

To this end, he walked over to Pommy, and holding her firmly by the shoulder with one hand, he dried her tears with his own handkerchief. "Now, now, my dear Pommy, you must not cry any longer! I am sure Mama has often said it is the ruination of one's complexion— if one is a lady, that is! Of course, men do not cry, but I should not think it would matter if they did, since their complexions are neither as delicate nor as important as those of ladies." He recollected his original purpose and continued eagerly, "Will you tell me whether the woman I love has any feeling for me at all?"

Unaware that this equivocal scene might be grossly misunderstood by the two persons approaching down the hallway, Pommy looked up into Gareth's beautiful, kindly, beef-witted countenance and a smile broke through her tears.

"Oh, Gareth, you are a darling! Of course I shall do exactly as you wish!"

In his delight at this wholehearted cooperation, Gareth gave his accomplice a hug, and bestowed upon her wet face a brotherly salute.

To Pommy's horror, Lady Masterson's voice rang out from the doorway at this instant.

"Why are you kissing Pommy, Gareth? Oh, are you in love at last?"

The culprits whirled to face her and found themselves also confronting a black-browed Derek. Lady Masterson had also turned to him.

"It is the answer to your problem, Derek! If we spread it about that Gareth is to marry Pommy, it will serve to discourage Mr. Corcran's unwelcome attentions." She smiled upon her son and his companion. "I shall arrange a small dance in Pommy's honor and invite Sally Jersey. The rumor will be all over London within twenty-four hours."

"But I do not—we do not—that is—" stammered the girl.

Lord Austell seemed to have himself well in hand again. "Quite a Romantic story, is it not, Pommy? Are you now playing Cinderella, or the Sleeping Beauty?"

"Neither," began Pommy desperately. "We do not—"

But with shocking perversity Gareth broke into her angry denial. "We'd be most grateful, Mama! Pommy shall help you with the guest list, shall you not—er—my dear?" and he made such an elaborate grimace toward the girl that the Earl's attention was arrested, and he stared hard at the white-faced Pommy.

Fourteen

WHEN GARETH, reminded gently by his mamà that he was missing his customary morning exercise, had gone off to ride in the Park, and Pommy, protesting that there was still much she wished to say, had been dispatched to ask Gordon to show her where the invitation cards were kept, Lady Masterson turned to confront her brother-in-law's ironic glance.

"Oh, yes, I know what you are thinking, Derek," she admitted, with a mischievous smile.

"I rather doubt that," replied the Earl, grimly.

"But I do! You are silently rating me for having pushed those two babies into a situation for which they have no liking, but I promise you I know what I am doing."

The Earl raised his eyebrows quizzically, but there was surprise in his expression. "So you realized there was nothing to matter in the rather adolescent exchange we witnessed?" he asked.

"More than that, I think I know where Gareth's real interest lies—but there are problems, Derek, and I cannot permit you to bustle into the affair like a male tornado, setting everyone heels over heads!"

Derek was forced to chuckle. "Now I wonder what schemes you are hatching in that devious brain of yours, my dear sister-in-law? Shall I be forced to come to your rescue?"

Aurora's laughter chimed musically. "You will have to wait, like Gareth and Pommy, for a full revelation at the appropriate time," she teased.

"You terrify me, Aurora," said Lord Austell not entirely facetiously. "And may I say that you delight me, as well? I have not seen you sparkle in this way for too long a time."

Lady Masterson stretched up her hand and patted the brown cheek gently. "Your diagnosis was correct, Dr. Austell," she jibed with soft eyes that belied her mocking voice. "Rx: one warm, sensitive, engaging girl, prone to Romantic fancies and too impulsively bent on carrying out harebrained schemes! Guaranteed to stir up a fresh interest in living in the most lachrymose of fashionable females!"

"If the prescription has succeeded, I am most grateful to the minx," Lord Austell said, and bent to kiss the slender white hand which had patted his cheek. It was thus that Pommy beheld them as she appeared outside the open doors of the drawing room, a large box of blank cards in her hands. She halted abruptly, smothered a startled "O!" and was turning hastily away when Lady Masterson caught sight of her.

"Do come in, Pommy. I am ready to jot down our guest list now, and you shall write out the invitations.

I understand you were educated by your grandfather, who was a notable scholar, so I am sure you write a very pretty hand." She smiled and seated herself at a *buhl escritoire.* "I shall draft a model for you."

Very conscious of Lord Austell's presence in the room, Pommy bent over Her Ladyship's shoulder as the latter's pen scratched swiftly across a card. The wording appeared to be in regular form until the last line, which said, "To meet Miss Melpomene Rand."

"But I am only your companion, Milady—!" the girl gasped. "You do me too much honor!"

"You are my medicine against melancholy," corrected Lady Masterson with a chuckle. "You have stirred me quite out of the doldrums. You must allow me to celebrate my new interest in living, my dear."

"I can see," commented the Earl wryly, "that I have been forgotten completely by my hostess. I shall therefore beg you to excuse me." He bowed to both ladies with his usual urbane charm and took his leave.

Pommy's eyes followed the tall, distinguished figure out of the room. She made herself fight against a wave of desolation. She had seen enough to convince her that her suspicions were correct. For all his disclaimer that Lady Masterson's shifting moods put him off, Lord Austell had been kissing her hand with such tenderness that it was impossible to mistake his feelings.

"She deserves him, too!" Pommy told herself loyally, remembering the unquestioning kindness with which her employer had received a perfectly strange young woman into her home, the distinguishing notice she had accorded to her, the lovely gowns purchased, and the insistence that Pommy accompany her on the pleasant little excursions to the dress shop and later to houses of her friends.

Still, Pommy did not succumb to maudlin self-sacrifice.

She was convinced that her own plan to get Gareth married to Isabelle was a sound one, since they were so equally matched in beauty, artlessness, and amiable stupidity, and since they were mutually heart-smitten. Singly, each would probably drive a future husband or wife to deadly boredom or frenzy, but as a couple they could well live a pleasant and rewarding life. Or so Pommy reasoned, and she was more than willing to assist the star-crossed lovers in any way possible. Since she was now inscribing the invitations to the Ball, she made sure that one was addressed to Isabelle—together with an impressive warning not to tell her father anything about it. She was not too sure that Isabelle would be able to follow such sensible advice, but left the matter in the hands of Fortuna, with a nod in the direction of the goddess Tyche as well. Then, feeling that she had done all in her power to placate both the Roman and the Greek Fates, she took an opportunity before dinner to tell Gareth what she had done, and warn him to be alert to attend Miss Boggs from the instant of her arrival.

"If you are seen to express partiality for *her,* it will not only prevent your being forced to offer for *me,* but it will also lessen the chances of Mr. Boggs's scheme against Lord Austell succeeding—do you see that?"

Gareth looked willing but doubtful.

"Miss Boggs could not be expected to marry both you *and* the Earl."

Gareth's face was suffused with color. It was obvious he was both shocked at the idea of his Isabelle marrying two men, and delighted to think that he might be one of them. Pommy gave him a benevolent pat upon the arm, and left him to his cogitations.

Knowing Lady Masterson's propensity for mischief, it should not have surprised Pommy when, after dinner, Her Ladyship announced quietly, "Be sure to send an invitation to Miss Boggs, dear child," and then gave her chiming laugh at the astounded faces of the two plotters. Then, forestalling questions, she inquired if Pommy had sent an invitation to Colonel Rand.

"I saw his name upon the list, ma'am," confessed Pommy, "but I was not sure ... the unfortunate situation—"

Lady Masterson interrupted breezily, "But my dear girl, surely it would be most improper for your engagement to be announced without a single member of your own family present? And from all I have heard, you would not really wish to see your Aunt Henga or her daughters after the way they have treated you!"

Though she dreaded bringing disappointment into that naughty, mischievous glance, Pommy said quietly, "I must insist that the idea of my becoming engaged to Gareth is embarrassing and inexpedient, Milady, and I cannot—"

"But of course it is, child," Aurora interrupted again, and this time her face was sweetly serious. She went on, "Inexpedient, that is. But I cannot quite see that anyone is being embarrassed. We have only said, 'To meet Miss Melpomene Rand.' How should that cause trouble for anyone? You must trust me, my dear. Perhaps it is difficult for you to do so, since you have so recently met me, but I must tell you that I feel you were sent to me at a time when my life was, through self-pity and weakness, drifting into a wasteland from which you have rescued me. You must see that I am now enjoying life with a zest I feared was forever lost to me?"

"If I have helped you in any way, Milady, I am happy," replied Pommy, torn between reassurance and a sense of guilt.

"Then you must be sure to send your dashing uncle-Colonel a card to your party," Lady Masterson charged her.

Pommy cast a searching glance upon her employer, and became aware of a becoming flush upon that lady's cheek and a new sparkle in the fine eyes which the girl did not think was put there by her new companion. She did hope that Uncle George would not turn awkward, but would be willing, for his niece's sake, to accept an invitation from the lady who had dismissed him so curtly on their first meeting! Pommy sighed deeply and got on with the invitations.

The day before the Ball, a new complication arose which threatened all Pommy's plans. It started very pleasantly at nine o'clock in the morning. At this very unfashionable hour, Chelm, the youngest footman, was on duty. Opening the door in response to a merry tattoo upon the knocker, Chelm found himself facing the largest bouquet of flowers he had ever beheld. When this was thrust into his arms, Chelm received it gingerly and peered around it to discover who had brought it. The donor was a rakish young Blade dressed to the nines and looking as fine as five-pence.

"Yers? Wotta you want?" he inquired warily, then, recalling Mr. Mikkle's tuition, added on, "sir?"

"I have come," said Alan Corcran blithely, for he was convinced he had fallen in love, "to pay my respects to Miss Rand."

"Miss Rand?" queried the footman suspiciously. Chelm himself had begun to harbor Romantic if admittedly impossible dreams in regard to Miss Pommy, and he disapproved of Corinthians and Rakehells making overtures to that young lady.

"Miss Rand," repeated the Blade, who was probably

a Corinthian and certainly a Rakehell. "Hop to it, my good man!"

Chelm's initial distrust hardened into acute dislike, and betrayed him into a remark which Mikkle would never have sanctioned.

"D'yer know wot time it is?"

Alan, who considered himself to be a regular Pink of the *Ton,* and up to all the rigs and rows, was naturally incensed by this piece of impertinence. "I should think it too early to expect visitors, if *you* have been put in charge of the door," he sneered. "Now take my flowers to Miss Rand and tell her I must see her about the matter we were discussing when last we talked." Then, adding insult to injury, he recapitulated his message slowly and clearly, as to a knock-in-the-cradle: "Flowers—to Miss Rand—say Mr. Corcran has information she needs."

Chelm, boiling with as black a sense of outrage as he had ever known, stalked off to the breakfast room where Pommy was lingering over a solitary cup of tea, Lady Masterson having given orders that no one was to disturb her before eleven o'clock. Naturally Pommy was pleased and impressed by the enormous nosegay, and her innocent delight further infuriated Chelm, who was sure the importunate caller had Designs on Miss Rand's virtue. When he had reluctantly delivered his message, he was forced to watch the girl flying out into the hall to welcome the visitor.

Pommy was so thankful to receive a young, uncritical, admiring caller after the Earl's cold strictures and quelling behavior, that she may have given Alan some ideas she did not intend. Chelm viewed this enthusiastic greeting with real foreboding. His darkest suspicions were confirmed when, on returning to his post, his ears shamelessly at the stretch, he overheard the girl agreeing to go out for a couple of hours in the Blade's new curricle, "where we can enjoy a private coze."

Pommy, not the green girl Alan hoped or Chelm feared, knew it was not *comme il faut* to be jauntering about London with a young reprobate in an open curricle, but her heart was sore from the Earl's frequently expressed disapproval, and she craved Alan's warmth and youthful high spirits.

Adjuring him to wait, she ran lightly up to her room and snatched up a saucy chip hat and her reticule. Upon impulse, she unwound her dark braid, which she was wont to wear twisted twice around her head like a coronet, and brushed it out into a glistening mane. Upon this she perched the chip hat. The fact that this made her look about ten years old did not reassure Chelm, who associated loose-flowing female hair with a special kind of confrontation. And now Miss Pommy was asking him to let Gordon know she had gone out for a couple of hours but would be back for lunch. Chelm reluctantly closed the door after them, cursing the young rep who was leading Miss P. astray.

In Alan's cheerful company it was easy for Pommy to forget her depression of spirit. After having said all that was fitting in admiration of the natty new curricle, she asked, "Where are we going?"

"I have learned there is a Fair outside the City, in a field," Alan replied, betraying a youthful enthusiasm at odds with his Man-of-the-Town pose. "I felt sure it would amuse you," he added, condescendingly.

"I am sure I shall enjoy it very much," said Pommy, "but I must be back in Portman Square by noon, you know. I am Lady Masterson's companion, you know, not a guest in her house."

Not much sobered by this caution, Alan, while agree-

ing to an early return, launched into a boyishly pompous dissertation upon the difference between the
ordinary companion to an elderly invalid and a young
woman lucky enough to have a Leader of the *Beau
Monde* as her patroness. "For it is easily seen," he said,
"that she does not regard you as a servant. What
servant accompanies her employer to the *Ton* parties,
dressed as you were at the Musical Evening?"

During the course of the drive, he let fall a good deal
about himself and his home in Surrey; his doting
parents and his own desire to be considered a Tulip of
the *Ton*. By the time the curricle drew up in a field
near the tiny Fair, Pommy had made a pretty sound
estimate of her cavalier's true nature, and was prepared to enjoy an innocent romp with him.

They found the Fair as much fun as Alan had promised. They played like two children, shouting with
laughter as they rode the swings, ups-and-downs, and
roundabout; throwing onions at targets, eating sau-
sage rolls in their fingers, and exclaiming over the
feats of the strong man and the ropewalker.

When Pommy reluctantly insisted they should return to Portman Square, Alan even more reluctantly
agreed. As they drew closer to the end of their adventure, Pommy said, "We have not had that private coze
you promised, you know."

Alan shrugged. "I would have said anything to get
you to come with me. It has been pleasant, has it not?"

"Delightful," said Pommy warmly. She was trying to
tidy the lustrous mane with her fingers, and get it
neatly settled under the absurd chip bonnet. Alan
grinned at her boyishly.

"You look a proper urchin, Pommy! Better get upstairs and brush your hair before Her Ladyship sees
you."

167

As he handed her down in front of Number Three, Alan gave the girl's slight body an extra swing before he returned her to her feet. She ran ahead of him up to the door, her face rosy with laughter, Alan in mock pursuit.

They were brought up short by the sight of a tall, elegant figure glaring at them from the open doorway.

"Lord Austell!" gasped Pommy.

For all his vaunted *nous* Alan could not face this confrontation. Muttering hasty goodbyes, he ran back to his curricle, mounted, and drove hastily away.

The Earl observed this craven retreat with a sardonic eye. "It is to be hoped that Mr. Corcran is more faithful in love than he appears to be dauntless in war," he said. "Or perhaps he has not read Mr. Scott's *Marmion*."

"We were having some fun at a Fair—" began Pommy, miserably conscious of her hoydenish appearance.

"Spare me your excuses," snapped the Earl. "I would suggest you attend to your appearance before presenting yourself to Lady Masterson! I beg leave to bid you good day!"

The Earl ran down the steps and strode rapidly away. Having spent a restless night afflicted with images of a pair of huge accusing green eyes, he had come to make his peace with Pommy this morning, only to learn from Chelm that Miss had run off with a queer nobs called Corker or some such. This news destroyed the indulgent mood with which he had prepared to inform the girl of the good fortune he intended to bestow upon her. The longer he waited, the less in charity he felt with the little wretch—but he consoled himself with the thought that after a morning spent with the insufferable Corcran, she would greet his own presence with joy. Instead of which, he found her romping childishly

168

with the cowardly youth, her glorious hair disheveled—
and having a perfectly wonderful time, if her laughing
little face was any warrant! Feeling very staid and old
and un-Romantic, the Earl, head high, made his disgruntled way down the street.

Fifteen

THE LONGER Alan Corcran thought about the situation at Number Three Portman Square, the more he became convinced that there was a Plot against Pommy. He was not exactly certain what his own feeling was toward the little companion of Aurora, Lady Masterson, but it seemed to be an incongruous blending of admiration, annoyance, desire, and a chivalrous wish to defend her from the rakehells and roués of London. Since, he supposed, he himself might be classed with the latter group, his protective attitude was all the more puzzling. He was forced to conclude, rather gloomily, that his rakish behavior since he came to London had been merely a wistful emulation of the real thing.

"It would seem I am not truly cut out for it," he told Todd, his valet, despondently.

"For what?" grumbled that worthy. Being a retainer who had been serving Corcrans before Alan was born,

Todd was not best pleased at the young sprig's aping of the Bucks and Corinthians, and had been heard to express the hope daily that Alan would tire of this damfoolery and let them both go home to Corcran Place where they belonged.

Alan had come to agree with him, but something in him would not permit him to leave young Pommy to her probably calamitous fate. He therefore sent a note to Number Three Portman Square, asking her to appoint a meeting in private. To this she replied that it was impossible for her to find free time, with her employer's social activities *in crescendo* as they were.

Alan's immediate response had been to seek information from some of his more sophisticated cronies. It was not hard to find—the *Ton* was agog over the piquant rumors which were circulating, each one wilder than its predecessors: The Lady Masterson had come out of her self-imposed seclusion at last, and was about to marry either a Duke or, if one accepted the word of a highly placed gossip, her own brother-in-law. Mr. Gareth Masterson was to be wed to Lady Masterson's companion, a mysterious female no one had ever heard of, said another of the intelligencers; and a member of Brooks's had been overheard to sneer that that impregnable Bastion of Bachelorhood, the Earl of Austell, had finally been caught out, and was to marry a tradesman's daughter.

His head buzzing with these piquant if contradictory *on dits,* Alan considered his priorities and determined to rescue Pommy from the clutches of the belted Earl. How to act upon this resolve presented another problem, for if he could not get admittance to talk to the girl, how was he to deliver her from the nefarious schemes of the Wicked Peer? It is to be feared that young Mr. Corcran was as great a Romantic in his own way as Pommy was in hers. His too-active imagination pictured the girl in a series of quite implausible situations, ranging all the way from elegant seduction to brutal rape. In a calmer mood, the young man would have greeted such lurid fantasies with a derisory grin, but his aplomb had been shaken by Mr. Boggs's initially successful if not conclusive attempt to lure him into parson's mousetrap, and his confidence in his own *savoir faire* had received a shock. For it was the promise of bigger game than a wretched second son of a minor Baron which had moved the vintner to inform Alan that his suit had been refused . . . a suit which he had not been aware he had pressed until so informed by Miss Boggs's papa, on the very afternoon of the day of the unfortunate party at which Isabelle had overheard his rather desperate jesting with his best friend.

Realizing with some emotion that it was past time he went back to his family's home in the country, he so informed Todd. "I have just one more piece of business to deal with here in London," he said. "You might as well pack everything. I do not fancy I shall wish to return to these lodgings."

"Oh, you'll be back, right enough," grumbled his valet, "if your father takes a house for the Season. What I want to know is, just when do you intend to leave?"

"I'll tell you after I've seen someone today," Alan promised, his mind more on the problem of rescuing Pommy from the results of her own ignorance than upon the unforgivably crusty behavior of his servant. Still cogitating deeply, he ordered Todd to bring round his new curricle. This natty vehicle was a gift from his loving parent, and had been the source of considerable pride to Alan. It quite outshone the very old-fashioned coach on which Todd had conveyed him and his luggage to London five months earlier. As he tooled the curricle neatly through the streets toward Portman Square, he kept working at the problem of Pommy. He did not have quite enough self-possession to call at Lady Masterson's mansion and demand to see the girl—Derek had done his work too well. But it suddenly occurred to the young man that he might knock at the door and ask that Miss Rand come out to the garden which was the central feature in the Square— to receive an urgent verbal message from home.

The ploy had a possibility of working, Alan decided, and proceeded to put it into action. Tethering his horses to a hitching post near the entrance gate to the garden, Alan walked across the road and delivered his message to a footman at Number Three. Then he made his way into the garden and sat upon a bench under a tree to await Pommy.

Within five minutes she came hurrying through the gate and down the path. Alan rose to greet her.

"What has happened?" she asked anxiously.

"I have been most worried about you, Pommy. I am about to return to my home in Sussex, and wished to assure myself that you were safe before I left."

Pommy smiled abstractedly. "What should cause you to worry, Mr. Corcran? I am happy and well occupied with my duties as Lady Masterson's companion, as you can see—"

"But that is not the word about Town," Alan contradicted her. "Rumor has it that you are to marry either Gareth or the Earl—"

"But that is nonsense," protested the girl, her color heightening.

"I should not have said so, seeing Austell's dog-in-the-manger attitude when last I called upon you!"

Alan stared at her rosy cheeks suspiciously. "But if it

173

is so, should you not consider the effects of such a baseless rumor upon your own reputation? There are only two courses of action which could prevent you from becoming one of the spiciest *on dits* of the Season!"

"What two courses?" Pommy was forced to ask.

"Either that the Earl should actually announce his engagement to you—and we both know how unlikely *that* is!—or that you should return at once to your own home and forget all this paltry, meretricious posturing which a group of idle fools with nothing really important to do call the Season," snapped Alan. His own failure to cut a swath as a dashing member of the *Ton* may have made him unnecessarily severe upon the glittering world he had not succeeded in conquering, but his words came to the girl with all the authority of a member of the Inner Circle. She caught her breath. It was worse than she had feared, then! The story was all over Town! But there was no way she could go home now. After the incident with Colonel Rand, it was more than likely that there would never be a welcome for her again at Highcliff Manor. Aunt Henga had made her return there impossible, with her cruel allegations. If not Highcliff, then where could she go? Pommy turned a face of dawning despair toward the young man.

"I cannot return home—it never was a real home to me, and now my aunt and uncle believe—believe—" she caught her breath in a sob. "Lady Masterson has been so good to me! I am sure the clothes she has bought me have cost far more than the salary I was to receive, so I cannot ask for any money—especially if I wished to use it to leave her!—and I have no means of providing for myself."

Alan nodded grimly. "They have tossed you into a rare bumble-bath, my poor girl! I had not realized you

174

had no other refuge. Yet I cannot see that you will do aught but worsen your situation if you remain and permit them to play off their tricks." He frowned heavily, holding his chin with one hand in such a boyish gesture that Pommy smiled even through her misery.

Then Alan clapped his hands together with a grin of relief. "I am a prize gudgeon!" he said cheerfully. "I am returning to my own home, Corcran Place, very soon—possibly tomorrow—and would like nothing better than to invite you to accompany me."

Pommy shook her head with the smile one reserves for charming children. "And I suppose your mama would be delighted to welcome a penniless, unknown female with no pretensions to fortune or family? You must be all about in your head, Mr. Corcran . . . but thank you for the kindly offer."

"Do you mean to stay on with Lady Masterson?" challenged Alan. "The word is about that startling announcements may be made on Friday night at the Ball."

"Oh, if only I knew more—if there was anyone I could ask!" muttered Pommy.

"What does Lady Masterson say to you about it all?" queried Alan.

"She tells me to wait and see . . . that I shall be surprised, 'pleasantly surprised'; that I must trust her," admitted the girl.

Alan shook his head. "I do not know Her Ladyship well—in fact she has been out of Society, I am told, for five years—but from all anyone says, she is a woman of good reputation, excessively devoted to her former husband."

"She has been kindness itself to me," cried Pommy. "I cannot believe she would be planning mischief!"

"Then you must just wait and see, must you not?"

was all the comfort Alan could offer. Soon after this inconclusive dialogue, Pommy hurried back into Number Three, and Alan mounted into his curricle, not at all satisfied with the turn of events. So dissatisfied was he that, before he reached his lodgings, he had hit upon a plan which he firmly believed would prevent any Deceivers, no matter how highly placed in Society, from playing off their tricks upon the guileless Miss Rand.

When Todd was informed of the plan, he behaved very much like a mule, stubborn, bad tempered and recalcitrant. "If you are asking me to help you with that totty-headed hocus-pocus, Mr. Alan, your wits have gone begging," he growled.

"I am not *asking* you," gritted Alan, regretting yet again that his father had insisted upon sending this old jobbernoll to London as his son's keeper, "I am *telling* you that this is what we are going to do! If you wish to go home, that is! For I shall not return to Corcran Place until I have seen Miss Rand safe out of London!"

Muttering direful prophecies of doom and disaster, Todd reluctantly allowed himself to be persuaded to aid in no less a connivery than the abduction of a maiden lady from one of the most elegant mansions in London, in broad daylight, on the afternoon of a Ball given in her honor.

Sixteen

THE EARL OF AUSTELL was also thinking deep thoughts about Miss Melpomene Rand and the Ball to be given in her honor. What the devil was Aurora playing at? It was not like his sister-in-law to run a rig on Society. He recalled, however, that when his brother had been alive, the pair of them had cut a wheedle or two which might well have set the *Ton* by the ears if he himself had not stepped in to make all right. But this latest start, giving a Ball for her young companion, was the outside of enough. The Earl did not begrudge Pommy her party; he was only afraid lest Aurora might place the girl in a position where she would receive the cut direct from certain high sticklers among London's *Haut Ton*. Smothering a curse, Lord Austell had himself driven round to Number Three Portman Square in full state: his coach with the crested panels, a liveried coachman and groom on the box, two up behind; himself dressed in his most impressive afternoon coat, and with what his brother had been wont to call his "Lord of the Manor, damn-your-eyes" look upon his handsome countenance. In the event, his state was wasted, since Lady Masterson was visiting her modiste, Mlle. Lutetie, and was not available for questioning.

Pommy, quickly notified by Mikkle via Gordon that His Lordship had honored them with his presence, made haste to present herself in the drawing room to accept whatever message Lord Austell wished to convey. She slipped so quietly into the room that the Earl was not immediately aware of her presence. Thus she was able to observe him unawares. She felt her heart swell in her chest at the sight of his stern dark countenance and superbly masculine figure. If only he had not seen her with Alan this morning!

Milord turned suddenly and caught her with her emotions displayed clearly in her lovely eyes. At once his expression softened and his smile of welcome made Pommy's pulse beat faster.

"My dear child! How charmingly you are looking!" He strode over to her and took her small hand in his large warm one. As he bent over it, the girl's eyes were drawn to the thick dark hair which curled on his well-shaped head, and she felt an almost overpowering urge to run her fingers through it. In a praiseworthy attempt to conceal the effect His Lordship was having upon her sensibilities, Pommy broke into hurried speech.

"Oh, Milord, Lady Masterson will be quite desolated to have missed you! I vow she was speaking only yesterday of the famous Balls and Ridottos you was used to give, and how everyone who had received an invitation was sure to come, which made all your parties the greatest squeezes—" She encountered his

178

quizzical look, one dark eyebrow raised, and had the grace to blush. "That sounded very silly, did it not?" she asked, in quite a different tone.

"Very," the Earl agreed. "Not at all like my Pommy. Why are you nervous of me? Is it because I caught you at your romp with Corcran?"

"I think," explained Pommy with disarming honesty, "it is because I am not sure what Lady Masterson intends to do about me at her Ball on Friday evening. And because I do not feel at all comfortable being singled out for notice as she has done on the invitations, by writing 'To meet Miss Melpomene Rand.' It frightens me, Milord. I am only her companion, with neither the background nor the desire to storm the citadel of London Society! Lord Austell, you must not let Lady Masterson try to force me upon the *Ton!*"

"You are afraid they will treat you with disdain?" queried the Earl with a frown.

Pommy brushed that aside. "I do not fear so much for myself—although I do anticipate personal embarrassment—for you know that I have not been accustomed to receiving excessive civility in my aunt's home. No, I fear that Lady Masterson will find her gracious effort to launch me into the *Beau Monde* received with mockery or contempt. I have come to know her, Milord; she has the gentlest, merriest nature, and she would be defenseless against malicious cruelty!"

The Earl studied the flushed little face of Lady Masterson's defender. "Do you think even the most vicious of harpies would openly attack a woman of Lady Masterson's consequence? Do not forget I shall be here also, and I am neither gentle nor defenseless where the honor of my House is under attack!"

Pommy's eyes held such adoration that the Earl caught his breath sharply. "No, Milord," she said, "I

179

believe the harpies would never dare to loose their venom directly upon your sister-in-law. Or any member of your family. But I am a different matter. They could imply, with justification, that I am thrusting myself in where I have no right to be. I think Lady Masterson would be hurt to see me snubbed. Oh, sir, can you not persuade her to let me remain in my room during the Ball? I am convinced no good can come of it! I cannot understand Her Ladyship's insistence!"

Since this speech echoed all Lord Austell's own doubts, he was compelled to admit the validity of Pommy's fears. He had not released her hand, nor had she sought to free herself from his firm clasp. Now he led her to a comfortable chair and bestowed her in it. Seating himself nearby, he said quietly, "I share your anxiety. You have given my sister-in-law a new interest, and she seeks, I am sure, to thank you for it in this way. It may be, also, that she hopes to promote a match between her son and yourself—no, do not shake your head, Pommy! Allow me to know Lady Masterson's generous nature and your own worth! You are well bred, of good country family, well educated, in every way but fortune a suitable match for Gareth—"

"We do not love one another," said Pommy in a small, clear voice.

The Earl smiled fondly at her, as one would at a beloved child or a lost dream. "Could Lady Masterson not hope that, in time, love might come? You are both so very young!"

"I am ages older than Gareth, Milord," retorted Pommy sternly, "and not beautiful enough to attract him. Nor is he—" she hesitated, unwilling to offend Gareth's uncle.

"Nor is he bright enough to attract you?" supplied the Earl wryly. "Yes, I take your point."

"Besides," Pommy added quickly, lest his feelings were hurt, "Gareth has already lost his heart to a beautiful and wealthy girl who thinks him to be the cleverest and most wonderful of men."

"He should secure such a treasure without an instant's loss of time." The Earl grinned. Then watching her intently, he prodded. "Does his mother know of this paragon? More importantly, does my nephew intend to confide in me? Such an important matter as the marriage of Mr. Gareth Masterson must not be left to Romantic caprice."

"He has fallen completely in love with Miss Isabelle Boggs," confessed Pommy. "And I assure you, they are—kindred spirits." She scanned his imperturbable face anxiously. "They would make each other extremely happy," she pleaded.

"Besides not spoiling two families," commented the Earl.

"Oh! How can you be so cruel?" cried Pommy. "Your own nephew!"

"You are attempting to convince me that either of them would not drive the average spouse to mayhem?" countered the Earl, with a wicked grin. He had been so sure that Pommy would be unable to resist the charm, beauty, and fortune of his nephew! Her attitude seemed to release a hard knot of depression within him, and he felt absurdly relieved and cheerful. "You must inform my sister-in-law of this delightful news as soon as she returns from her round of shopping," he advised the frowning girl. "Tell her also that the match has my full approval, since it releases me completely from the threats of Mr. Boggs. Remind her also that it will probably serve to accomplish her dearest wish, since the Boggs child is even more biddable than Gareth,

181

and Aurora can probably command their attendance upon her until they are ninety!"

Pommy was not pleased at the Earl's unseemly levity. "Are you saying you will not object to the connection with Mr. Boggs?" she queried.

"Better he should be Gareth's papa-in-law than mine." The Earl laughed heartily, with what Pommy felt was cruel indifference. Still, he might have a point. She was forced to admit that Gareth was not subtle or sensitive enough to find Mr. Boggs's crudities offensive. And she had a pretty good idea that the Earl would be able to depress the vintner's pretensions and keep him in line. Pommy sighed.

"Then there is no reason for me to appear at Lady Masterson's Ball," she urged. "I would *really* rather not, Milord!"

But the Earl was cock-a-hoop, and greeted her earnest plea with a twinkling smile. "What, Faint Heart! Have you no sense of the Romantic? Who knows what thrilling adventures will befall you, like Cinderella at the Ball? I am coming to think that my dear sister had a better idea than I understood!"

"Oh, you are impossible!" snapped Pommy unforgivingly, and ran from the room, followed by the Earl's joyous laughter.

Seventeen

THE MORNING of the Ball dawned clear and bright. Birds tootled merrily in the trees in Portman Square. Lady Masterson was in alt. Her mood of elation was so much like Lord Austell's that Pommy wondered if the whole family was subject to sudden onsets of high spirits. The servants, too, were affected; It was obvious that they were delighted to rouse from their long hibernation and reenter the glittering Social World again.

Lady Masterson summoned Pommy to her dressing room, where Gordon was hastily arraying her in a charming morning gown.

"You must not overtire yourself, Milady," cautioned the girl.

Aurora laughed. "I have seldom been so happily engaged as I have been with the plans for this evening," she said.

Indeed, Pommy thought, her employer had been too much absorbed with her plans for the special orchestra, the sumptuous refreshments, and the unusual *décor* to be conscious of the fatigue normally enjoyed by Society Hostesses. Her catch phrase—"It must be the best party of the Season!"—had been adopted by all her well-paid and devoted staff, so happy to see their beautiful mistress herself once more that they accomplished prodigies for her.

The huge ballroom had been transformed into a charming grotto, complete with a waterfall and hundreds of flowering shrubs and ferns in pots. All six of the French doors were set wide open to the coolth and fragrance of the gardens, admittedly smaller than the Earl's but sweet with the scents of flowers. The broad terrace outside the ballroom had been waxed so that the guests might dance there in the Romantic light of flambeaux.

Card rooms were made ready for those who had no wish to dance. At three separate buffets, champagne, fruit punch, and other cooling beverages were to flow as lavishly as the decorative waterfall. The house sparkled and gleamed, waiting to welcome Lady Masterson's guests.

Lord Austell dropped by before noon to present Her Ladyship's butler with a dozen cases of champagne and three of a brandy which had Mikkle beaming. Milord refused Lady Masterson's invitation to remain for lunch, claiming that he must get his beauty sleep before dinner in order to look his best at the Ball.

When he had departed, laughing like a boy, Aurora raised her eyebrows at Pommy. "I do not think I have ever seen Derek so lighthearted! If I did not know better, I should suppose he had fallen in love. But of course, at his age . . ."

Pommy, unaccountably cross, had to exert strong control to prevent herself from making a tart reply. She was by now fairly sure that the hilarity which had seized both the Earl and Her Ladyship was the effect of their falling in love—with each other. If anyone had found himself in love with her, and she with him, Pommy knew she would experience just that wonderful sense of elation which Derek and Aurora were bubbling with. She told herself she was happy for them and that the match was most suitable as to age, fortune, and preeminence in Society.

As the day dragged toward its climax, her feeling of dread increased. Even the darling dress which Gordon brought to her after lunch—a gift from her generous employer—could not raise her spirits from the gloomy depths into which they had fallen. Gordon, looking askance at the pale face and heavy eyes of the girl she had come to like and respect, tried to interest her in the delicate flowers wrought in silver thread upon the white silk.

"It seems to be made of moonlight," offered the Dragon in a rare flight of fancy.

Pommy admitted that it was beautiful and then burst into tears.

"Now then, Miss Pommy, that is no way for you to behave!" protested Gordon.

"I am not worthy of all this kindness and attention!" sobbed the girl. "It frightens me!"

Gordon had been briefed by Lady Masterson, who had learned a good deal from the Earl about the treatment Pommy had received at Highcliff Manor, including the slapping and the enforced journey in the rain. She muttered now that she knew what she would like to do to the old harridan and her nasty daughters. At this evidence of strong partisanship, Pommy raised tear-filled eyes and asked, "What old harridan, Gordon?"

"Your aunt," replied the outspoken dresser crisply. "Miss Pommy, it is like the story about the girl who had to sweep up the ashes. The old woman and her two ugly daughters always so cruel, and poor Cinderella so sweetly pretty—and forever being put upon! I would know what to say to them!"

"My cousin Ceci is very pretty," said Pommy, striving to be fair but already comforted.

"Pretty is as pretty does," replied Gordon darkly. "I've seen her sort! All smiles and big eyes when the men are around, and a regular viper to her maid."

"Oh, Gordon, I do like you!" cried Pommy, and gave the gratified dresser a hug.

"Well, you'll please me most if you lie down and rest now, with a wet cloth over your eyes. All that crying has made them red, and you must look your best tonight, Cinder-pommy!"

Smiling at her own wit, Gordon hung up the new dress in the armoire and went softly from the room. She knew as well as the girl that the tears had not been shed over the unloving relatives, but for love of six feet four inches of virile manhood—but like Pommy, she would never admit to it.

Pommy did lie down for half an hour, but she was not accustomed to sleeping in the daytime, and the sounds of activity from the lower floors, though subdued, kept her alert. At length she rose, washed her face, and stealing just one quick peek inside the armoire at the white and silver gown, she went down to see what she could do to help with the preparations.

While she was crossing the great main hall, there was an assault on the knocker, and a footman in a baize apron hurried to open the door. On the threshold stood a small, stocky man dressed in sober black, evidently someone's servant bearing a message. Pommy came forward to accept the information. But instead of an acceptance or regret for the Ball, the message was for her personally, as the little man soon informed her.

"That's all right, Chelm." Pommy smiled at the harassed footman. "You can go back to whatever you were doing. It is only a note for me."

But when she opened it (for the little man stood glumly on the porch, awaiting her reply), Pommy had a sudden wave of shock which made her momentarily dizzy. The note was signed "Isabelle," and read as follows:

Dearest Pommy: When you read this you must say *absolutely nothing* to *anyone.* You must get your reticule and a cloak and *come* with the messenger to where I am being *held. Only you* can *save* me. Do *not* betray my *trust!*

Pommy raised her eyes to the dour little servant. "What—?"

"Say nothing," he ordered, pointing to the note.

But Pommy was made of sterner stuff than that.

"Is it an abduction?" she whispered. "Should I not obtain money? For the ransom?"

Looking as though he thought that might be a very good idea, the little man reluctantly shook his head. "Get yer cloak an' bag. You won't be hurt," he advised sourly. Pommy had the distinct impression that this whole theatrical performance was highly distasteful to him. His manner reassured the girl. She went swiftly up the stairs for her cloak and reticule. After a moment's thought, she placed a small, sharp pair of scissors in her bag (useful for stabbing attackers or cutting ropes), and three extra handkerchieves (remembering Isabelle's penchant for easy tears). Finally she added all the money of which she was possessed, a paltry sum, since she had not yet received a wage, but which might help to bribe someone, or hire a coach. Then she slipped down the great stairs, thinking herself fortunate not to encounter anyone in a position to challenge her.

Waiting outside the closed front door was the little man. Pommy now observed a small enclosed coach standing a few doors down the street, with a well-muffled coachman upon the box. The little servant led her to this coach, assisted her to enter, closed the door after her, and clambered up beside the coachman. They were off with a jerk and a scraping of iron-shod hooves upon the cobbles.

Pommy sank back into the gloomy depths of the musty old cab. She had time now for second thoughts, and began to wonder if she had not behaved with consummate folly. She fumbled in her reticule for Isabelle's note, only to realize with dismay that it was not there. She tried to recall where she had put it, but nothing emerged from the jumble of her recollection. Pommy sighed. Well, perhaps one of the maids would pick it up and throw it in the dustbin. Few of them were able to read, so it was unlikely they would be concerned over the rather grubby little scrap of paper. Pommy closed her eyes and tried to restore the tone of her mind, in preparation for whatever challenge awaited her.

At this moment Lady Masterson was absorbing the contents of Isabelle's note with distended eyes. Chelm, who had opened the door to the little man, had a very soft spot for Miss Pommy, and had liked neither the effect of the message upon the girl, nor the cut of the messenger's jib. When, hovering near the door to the main hallway, he had observed Miss Pommy first run upstairs and then come racing down, he had been alarmed. He noticed the small white paper which had fluttered to the floor as Pommy shut the little man outside the front door, and had whipped out of concealment to snatch it up before the girl could return. He himself was not a skilled reader, being, in fact, limited to forming his own name and deciphering the numbers and letters on currency, but he was impressed by the underlinings and by Miss P.'s reception of the contents. He therefore took the letter at once to Lady Masterson's suite, and handed it, with a brief explanation, to Gordon. He lingered long enough in the hallway to hear Her Ladyship's shriek of dismay, and then returned to his work, confident that he would be called upon speedily to tell his tale.

This was indeed the case. When he had explained every detail of the event to Her Ladyship, he was sent with an urgent message to Lord Austell's home. While Lady Masterson nervously awaited the arrival of her brother-in-law, another servant brought the information that Colonel Rand was below and wished to have a word with his niece.

"O God!" shrieked Lady Masterson, her appalled gaze flashing to Gordon. "We have lost Pommy! He will hate me!"

The Dragon, who knew more than her mistress gave her credit for, promptly offered to see the colonel and explain the situation.

"But how can you, Gordon, when we don't understand it yet ourselves?"

"Then I think you must receive the gentleman yourself, Milady, and tell him what we do know," urged

Gordon. "You are in great good looks this morning, and that violet muslin really brings out your eyes. Shall you receive him in the drawing room?"

"No, for you know as well as I do that the servants are thronging through all the lower rooms, giving them a last minute polish," cried the distracted lady.

"Then I shall have to bring him here," announced Gordon with barely concealed satisfaction. It was past time, she thought, that a masculine boot trod the charming delicacy of the mauve and rose carpet, and a masculine eye observed the exquisite beauty of Her Ladyship in such a setting.

Lady Masterson had scarcely time to compose her features and apply a little of her French perfume before Gordon deposited the colonel. Her Ladyship shyly raised her eyes to his bold, commanding countenance. What she saw there went a good way toward restoring her confidence. For the colonel, no ladies' man, was bowled over by the fragrant femininity before him. His hard eyes almost goggled at the sight of this adorable woman in such an intimate setting. Feeling extremely crass and heavy footed, he marched forward across the delicate carpet as though he were walking upon eggs, and bent with a military precision to kiss her soft white hand. His rout was completed when her soft voice breathed above his head in anguished tones:

"Oh, my dear sir, you will be terribly angry with me, but indeed, Colonel Rand, I could not prevent it!"

The colonel straightened his big, battle-hardened body and stared into the most enchanting countenance it had ever been his pleasure to set eyes upon. Gone was the haughty *grande dame* who had spurned him so coldly. This was a warm and frightened woman, for whom the colonel's chivalry was immediately enlisted.

"Whatever is troubling you, Lady Masterson, I shall never blame you. Only tell me what I can do to help you!"

Lady Masterson indicated a chair close to her *chaise longue,* and they seated themselves in silence. Then, gathering up her courage, she told him the facts as she knew them.

"But how is this a fault in you?" the gallant colonel asked. "My niece received a letter from a friend; she left in answer to that friend's appeal. You knew nothing of it until the message was discovered. I shall go round to Miss Boggs's residence at once and see what the trouble may be."

"I fear that Pommy has been decoyed away by kidnappers," said Aurora, her tear-filled eyes abject upon his face. "And while she was in my care, too! It is shaming—"

"Nonsense," the colonel said briskly. "From the way she looked when last I saw her—" he hesitated, noted the rosy flush which crept across the white cheeks, and took firm control. "No, Milady, we must not permit ourselves to dwell upon *that* unhappy occasion. Tempers were short. An unpleasant woman had made mischief. But I saw for myself that the girl was happy and comfortable in your gracious care—"

"From which she has been decoyed!" Aurora persisted, enjoying the pleasure of his reassurances.

"Through no fault of your own," the colonel reminded her, and was emboldened to lean forward enough to clasp her hand. This she seemed willing enough to relinquish into his grasp, and for a moment neither of them spoke. Then, with a final gentle pressure, the colonel released it reluctantly, and resumed the discussion. "What measures have been taken so far?" he asked.

"I have sent for Lord Austell," began Her Ladyship. "I—I had not thought to send for you, sir," she apologized.

The officer rose and strode around the room as though feeling the need for action. "Good! Your brother-in-law will be aware of the friendship between my niece and Miss Boggs, since I am given to understand that it was he who brought both of them to you in London. He will therefore have Miss Boggs's direction. I shall accompany him to the Boggs residence."

Lady Aurora was suddenly struck by another thought. "Why did you come here today, Colonel Rand? I was informed you wished to speak to your niece."

A softened look came into the soldier's face. "I had bought a gift for her—a trifle to wear at your Ball—which I am sure, knowing my sister-in-law Henga, is the first she has ever attended! I was going to make sure she had a pretty dress, too," he confessed with some embarrassment, hoping that this honest statement would not anger his niece's employer.

On the contrary, Lady Masterson smiled at him with such approval that his heart began to pound in his chest. "That was thoughtful of you, sir! And are you very knowledgeable in the matter of ladies' gowns?" she teased.

This sally gratified him enormously, as she had intended it should do, and while he made a suitable disclaimer, she was pleased to note that the warm look was still present in his eyes, and softened his hard features enormously.

"What trinket had you brought for Pommy? Will you show it to me," she invited, "since we must wait for Austell to take you to Miss Boggs's residence?"

The soldier took from an inner pocket a small white jeweler's box. Opening it, he displayed a small string of perfect pearls.

"Exquisite," pronounced Her Ladyship. "Most suitable for a young girl in her first Season."

The colonel frowned. "That is something I had hoped to discuss with you, Lady Masterson," he began. "I am most grateful for what you are doing for my niece, but I am not quite certain how matters stand. She is your companion, is she not? Surely you do not intend to sponsor her into the *Ton?*"

Whatever Lady Masterson might have confided to this very masterful soldier will never be known, for at that very moment Gareth burst into her sitting room in a positive frenzy of alarm. Completely ignoring the unusual sight of a large military gentleman seated upon one of his mama's dainty chairs, he shouted, "What has happened to Isabelle? Where is Pommy? Oh, why was I not summoned?"

His mama regarded her agitated son with disfavor. "We are already doing all we can until Derek arrives to take the colonel to Miss Boggs's home," she said sternly. "You will bring on a headache with this uproar."

"I never have headaches," said Gareth simply.

"I do, however, upon occasion," said his mother repressively, "and I do not wish this to be one of them. You seem to forget that we are having a large formal Ball this evening."

"Not if Isabelle is missing!" protested Gareth.

"What has Miss Boggs to say to anything?" asked his mother coolly.

"I love her," retorted Gareth. "I shall accompany my uncle and Colonel Rand to search for her."

"Oh, in that case," agreed Lady Masterson, softening toward her son. "Of course, if you love her—*you love her!*" she shrieked, suddenly taking in what he had said.

"I intend to marry her, and settle down—"

193

"My son!" breathed Her Ladyship. "You are fulfilling my fondest hopes for you! You shall both live here, and be my dear companions—"

"You already have Pommy for that," said Gareth, setting his beautiful mouth stubbornly. "I wish Isabelle to come with me to my own estate."

"You would leave your mother alone—?" began Lady Masterson, a desolate expression clouding the delicate beauty of her face.

"Lady Masterson," interrupted Colonel Rand urgently, "*dearest* Lady Masterson! Never while I live shall you be left alone! Only say that you permit me to court you—that you will listen to my representations—that is, that I may be allowed to offer for you—" He took out an immaculate handkerchief and wiped his forehead. "Lady Masterson!" he ended upon a note of desperation.

The lady so passionately apostrophized bent upon her petitioner a speculative glance. It suddenly occurred to her that a gallant officer with matrimony in mind might be a far better attendant than a love-smitten son or even a love-smitten companion. She gave the distressed officer a gentle smile, whose demureness was belied by the provocative twinkle in her lovely eyes.

"Although I had not realized it until the advent of your dear niece, I find I am becoming bored with living retired," she admitted. "I should expect you to engage in an active social life with me—that is, of course, if I were to accept your proposal."

Such a light dawned upon the soldier's stern face that even Gareth was struck by it.

"If you were—! Oh, My Lady, could you ever consent—?"

"An *active* social life," insisted His Lady, striking while the iron was hot.

The dazzled soldier would have sworn his head was his heels at that moment. To gain the prize he had dreamed of since their first calamitous meeting, with only the stipulation that he should take this radiant being into Society upon his arm, seemed to the besotted creature no penalty at all, but the utmost delight.

"It would be my deepest pleasure to escort Your Ladyship to every reception and Ball in London," he promised, eyes on her adorable face.

"I shall hold you to that, sir," Lady Masterson warned him happily.

"Unless, of course, we become engaged in another war," amended her colonel conscientiously. "In which case I might be called overseas."

"We shall face that when we come to it," agreed Aurora silkily. Secretly she had already decided that if another conflict broke out before Colonel Rand was too old to go to it, she would pull whatever strings were necessary to have him stationed at the War Office in London.

Gareth watched the two happy faces with satisfaction. He was beginning to see that this union would release him from social duties he had come to find more than irksome, free him to take his Isabelle to—*his* Isabelle? Why were they not out searching for her? His panic was only allayed by the entrance, at that moment, of Lord Austell. The Earl at once assumed command of the situation.

"I am sure you are wishful to come with me to Miss Boggs's home, Rand," he began. "Chelm has put me into the picture as we drove here. I have some suspicions that all is not exactly as it appears, but our first step is naturally to go to Isabelle's residence."

"I am coming with you," announced Gareth. One look at his stubborn face convinced the Earl not to waste time arguing.

"Very well. My carriage is at the door. Let us leave at once. I shall take Chelm with me, Aurora, since he seems to have his wits about him, and can recognize the servant who brought the note. I'll send him back to you as soon as there is anything to report. Meanwhile, do not succumb to the vapors, I implore you!"

Leaving her smiling wryly, he was about to lead the way downstairs when he noticed Colonel Rand hanging back long enough to plant a firm kiss upon Milady's rosy lips, which startled her as much as it delighted her. *No slow-top, the soldier,* though the Earl, as the colonel, brick-red but defiant, met his raised eyebrows. "Your servant, Lady Masterson." The colonel bowed. Then, "I am with you, sir," he told Lord Austell.

Within fifteen minutes the Earl's carriage drew up in front of the vintner's lavish residence. To Gareth's delight and the other men's dismay, Miss Isabelle was discovered to be safely within, and had no knowledge of anything remotely connected with the sensational material in the scrubby letter which the Earl produced.

"But of course I did not write that!" she said. "I would be ashamed to send out such a wretched scrawl! I cannot think what this is all about."

"It is a trick to lure Pommy away from my sister's home," said the Earl grimly. "We have now to decide who is villain enough to perpetrate such a wicked hoax."

"Her aunt?" suggested both Isabelle and George Rand.

"Possibly—although this does not have quite the sound of a disgruntled, essentially prosaic female," Lord Austell objected. "It has rather a Romantic sound—"

"You are suggesting that Pommy sent this to herself?" queried Colonel Rand, bristling.

"Of course not," snapped the Earl. "For one thing, Chelm admitted the messenger, and he has already told us how white Pommy became as she read the note. No, this is the work of someone with quite a different kind of Romantic imagination than our Pommy's. But who wrote it," he added severely, "is not our first concern. Where is Pommy? That is what I wish to know!"

"Do you think it is abduction for ransom?" ventured Isabelle, who was already weeping without appreciable change in her flawless features. Gareth rushed across the room to comfort her, while the Earl said decisively:

"No, I think not. Chelm said Pommy offered to get money, and the messenger rejected the offer."

"Then why—?" asked Colonel Rand in bewilderment. "The whole affair has a very amateur taint."

"Exactly." The Earl looked grim. "The writer of that note knew exactly how things stood between Miss Isabelle and our Pommy—that they were friends, and that Pommy, Romantic idiot that she is, would rush unheeding upon her fate if offered the challenge of a friend's distress."

"Someone who knows her well, then," agreed the colonel. "Miss Isabelle, do you have knowledge of any young man who might consider himself sufficiently enamored of Pommy to wish to spirit her away in this manner?"

Isabelle shook her lovely head. "I was not aware that Pommy knew any young men in London, aside from Mr. Gareth Masterson and Mr. Corcran—"

"Corcran!" snapped the Earl. "He's hanging out for a rich wife, is he not? Was he not dangling after you until your father changed his mind?"

"Really, Lord Austell, you speak too freely," said Rand stiffly. Gareth was glaring angrily at his uncle. Isabelle stared from one to another of the gentlemen with an expression of bewilderment upon her flawless face. The Earl ignored them all.

"Corcran must know Pommy hasn't a groat," he said tensely. "There must be some other reason he's abducted her. Did he have a *tendre* for her, do you know, Miss Isabelle?"

"He ain't plannin' *marriage* if he's run orf with 'er," Chelm spoke for the first time from his position on the fringe of the group.

"What the devil are you all talking about?" asked Gareth. "What makes you think Pommy has gone off with Alan Corcran?"

Isabelle had disregarded everything except the Earl's question. She was thinking hard, and after a moment she said to Lord Austell, "Pommy had lost her heart to someone, I am sure of it. But I cannot recall her mentioning the man's name. I suppose it could have been Mr. Corcran."

"Then in that case," said the Earl heavily, "we need not interfere."

"The devil we won't!" snapped Colonel Rand. "I have no intention of permitting my niece to compromise herself with some fortune-hunting rascal who lures her away from Lady Masterson's care with lying letters purporting to come from Miss Boggs! Where is this scoundrel's lodging?"

"He will not be there," said the Earl. "Chelm said there was baggage upon the coach in which they drove away."

"His people have a place somewhere in the country," began Gareth. "I'm sure I've heard him mention it.

Shropshire or Sussex ... wait, it's called Corcran Place and it's in—in—"

"Well, *remember!*" commanded the Earl more harshly than he had ever before addressed his heir.

"*Surrey!* That's it!" announced Gareth with considerable satisfaction. "I was sure I should get it!"

The Earl marshaled his forces. "Rand, I shall want you with me. You are the girl's closest relative, and can make our position unassailable. Gareth, go at once to Portman Square and acquaint your mother with the details of our plan—"

"But I don't know them!" protested Gareth.

"God give me strength," groaned the Earl.

The colonel, who, through his years in the army, was more used to dealing with young beef-brains than was Lord Austell, took smooth charge.

"Masterson!"

"Yes?" asked Gareth, and then catching the colonel's eye, "sir?"

"First. You will inform Her Ladyship that Austell and I have gone after Miss Pommy. Second. Miss Pommy is with Mr. Alan Corcran. Third. We shall have my niece back to Portman Square this evening. Is that clear?"

Gareth frowned as he mentally rehearsed the information. A smile broke over his handsome features. "Oh, yes! But are you sure—?"

"That is our problem, sir, not yours," Colonel Rand told him firmly. "Go now. Do you know the way from here? Walk back with Chelm. We shall need the Earl's carriage."

"Yes, sir," said Gareth, smiled at his uncle, bowed gracefully over Isabelle's hand, and made smartly for the door, following Chelm.

The Earl exhaled deeply and took his admiring gaze

from the commanding officer. "Miss Isabelle, do not be alarmed. Gareth will be quite safe with Chelm. So will Pommy, for we shall find her. Have you received an invitation to Lady Masterson's Ball?"

"Oh, yes!" Isabelle dimpled with pleased anticipation.

"Then you will see Gareth there, and can reassure yourself of his well-being. We must take our leave of you now, for Mr. Corcran has at least an hour's start on us, and if we don't discover his address soon—"

"Oh, I should think you could easily reach Dorking before dark," interjected Isabelle.

"Dorking?" repeated the men in unison.

Isabelle smiled sweetly. "That is where Corcran Place is located. Alan often spoke of it," she explained.

Once again in Lord Austell's carriage, the two men stared at one another.

"I shall never be able to understand women," confessed the colonel at last. "Why didn't she mention it earlier, when Gareth was trying so hard to remember? She knew it all the time!"

"I suppose," said the Earl, beginning to smile, "because nobody asked her. In any event, it's saved us hours of fruitless search. Let us be grateful she mentioned it at all!"

They were soon bowling along smartly on the south road out of London, each man silently absorbed in his own plans.

Eighteen

POMMY BECAME AWARE that the musty, old-fashioned coach in which she was riding was making its way out of London. The westering sun was ahead and on her right, so she assumed they were heading to the south. She began to wonder if she had not been stupid to place herself quite so trustfully in the power of the queer old man. She wished she had kept Isabelle's letter in her hand; she might have learned something from a more careful perusal of it. She was becoming disgusted with her lack of quick-wittedness, and even a little apprehensive as to her destination, when the coach creaked to a halt beside a small inn nearly covered with green vines. The coachman swung down and came quickly around to open the door for her. She found herself staring into the smiling face of Alan Corcran.

Instead of the pleased recognition which the young

man obviously expected, Pommy regarded him as though she would like to do him an injury. Her first words confirmed this.

"Alan Corcran! How dare you play off your tricks and frighten me so! I could strike you! What have you done with Isabelle?"

Considerably taken aback, Alan replied, "I have done nothing with her. I would suppose she is at her home, where she may stay, for all of me." He scowled at her. "I had thought you would be excessively grateful to me!"

"Grateful?" echoed Pommy in accents of scorn. "I am hungry, exhausted by a long drive in this miserable excuse for a carriage, half out of my mind with anxiety over Isabelle's fate—and you say I should be grateful? I think you must be the greatest blockhead in nature!"

Angry color rose in Alan's face. "And this is the thanks I am to receive for saving your honor! I might have expected it! My father was right."

"Your father? What has he to say to this? Did he advise you against this ridiculous rig you are running? You would have been wiser to have heeded him."

"My father," said Alan coldly, "is forever reading to Mama and me from his favorite poets. It is one reason I came to London. This situation, however, puts me strongly in mind of his favorite couplet:

Of all the plagues with which the world is cursed,
Of every ill, a woman is the worst!"

"Your mama is to be pitied," said Pommy repressively.

They kept glaring at one another until Todd, leaning out from the coachman's seat, said crossly, "I told you how it would be, Master Alan. Now do go inside and order some food, and I'll drive Miss back to London before her fine friends have the Runners after us!"

Pommy thrust the door open wider, nearly knocking Alan down. As he staggered away from the coach, she got out herself and stood facing him.

"You shall not fob me off with this Machiavellian servant of yours, *Master* Alan! I am starving. Order food for me, too, and then you may hire a carriage to take me back to Portman Square."

"Language!" muttered the scandalized Todd, misliking the sound of "Machiavellian." "In my day, well-brought-up young misses did not use such terms—"

"In *your* day, it is to be hoped that well-brought-up young misses were not raped from their homes and protectors by hardened rakehells, nor deceived by lying appeals for help purporting to come from their friends!"

Todd, who was now thoroughly alarmed by the word "rape" uttered in a loud clear voice in a public place, cast a piteous look at his young master, who had, after all, landed the two of them in this bumble-broth. "Oh, lordie me, what's to do, Master Alan?"

Put somewhat on his mettle by the abject surrender of his crusty henchman, Alan tried to retrieve the situation.

"Come, Pommy, this is the veriest fustian, and you know it," he offered coaxingly. "You will realize, if you will pause to give it a moment's reflection, that I thought I was saving you from great embarrassment at Lady Masterson's Ball tonight. My intention was to take you to my mother's home, where you might safely reside until your future had been secured—"

"Are you telling me that your own mama is privy to this outrageous abduction?"

Alan had the grace to look apologetic. "Well, I have not had time to consult her, in actual fact, but," catching sight of Pommy's glare of disgust, "but I *know* she would never reject anyone I brought to her. As boys, my brother and I were forever bringing home stray puppies and kittens—"

It did not take Todd's groan of exasperation to tell Alan he had not mended matters. "This is the outside of enough!" raged Pommy. "Stray puppies, is it? You have more than likely ruined my reputation, lost me my position, and made it ineligible for any decent person to speak to me—and you dare to aver that you thought you were saving me from embarrassment?"

By this time, the small group of servants and rustic idlers who had been attracted by the sounds of a heated altercation was beginning to take sides and express either supportive or opposing views. There were some pretty severe looks cast at the young Blade in the dandified raiment, as well as a disapproving glance or two at the young lady who was raising her voice against the gentleman. In the face of this concerted interest, the combatants felt it would be more dignified to continue their argument under more private circumstances, and repaired to the inn dining room in a state of armed truce.

Alan at once ordered a substantial meal to be served in some private room with all speed, since he and his party were too hungry to wait. Their host regretted that he had no private rooms such as young smarts from London might be accustomed to, but the public dining room being empty at the moment, as any fool could plainly see, since it was past four o'clock, and all normal persons had already dined, the public dining room, he repeated, gathering the thread of his somewhat discursive speech, should suffice their needs if they would be good enough to sit down in it.

Alan, resenting the implied slurs upon himself which

he was sure he discerned in the rambling oration, was about to carry the battle further when Todd and Pommy together pulled him down into a chair at the table, and Pommy said crisply, "Serve the meal, Host!"

Alan rattled back gamely, saying he was well aware what o'clock it was, since he was famished to the point of tipping somebody a doubler if he didn't get his mutton pretty promptly.

"Oh, don't be such a gudgeon," snapped Pommy. "The man's gone to the kitchen, and can't hear you, which is just as well, for we'd never have gotten anything to eat if you'd kept on haranguing him!"

Naturally this remark did not endear her to Alan, who subsided into a fuming silence, nor to Todd, who was heard to mutter something about women being seen but not heard. When the meal was served, it was quite good, and the three travelers ate in silence. Pommy made the first move toward a renewal of hostilities.

"Is it true, as I suspect, that Isabelle knew nothing of this rig you are running?"

"I had only hoped to save you from shame," retorted Alan bitterly.

"There may be something to your fears," Pommy was forced to concede. "I have no idea what amiable folly Her Ladyship has the intention of committing tonight. I am sure it has something to do with me, for she has urged me repeatedly to trust her."

"Unnerving," agreed Alan, a little less morosely.

"But how can I?" continued the girl. "I do not at all understand persons of her order, having met none of them until just lately. The nobility seems to be capable of any lunacy!"

"What did you think she might do?" asked Alan with rising interest.

"Well, for a time I believed she might be trying to arrange a marriage between myself and Gareth, but that is quite ineligible on at least two counts."

"What are they?" Alan was now completely absorbed in the drama.

"For one, Gareth is smitten with Isabelle."

"No!" breathed Alan. "He would bore most women out of their wits!"

"Yes, well, they find each other all that is delightful, and I am persuaded they would go on very well together. The second objection to the connection is that I have none of the qualities nor the attributes which would make me a suitable *parti* for such a nobleman."

"I don't see that—" Alan began to protest, but Pommy raised a hand.

"We are dealing honestly now with one another, Alan, since I may need to beg the assistance of a small loan from you before we part—to be repaid with interest, of course."

"It is no more than I owe you," admitted Alan handsomely, "after snatching you away from your home in that way."

"Thank you," said Pommy. "Now as to my unsuitability for marriage to a nobleman. I am the daughter of a third son—"

"That's worse than me," said Alan feelingly.

"I have no portion, nor hope of any. I have a classical education, but that can be counted as a drawback rather than an asset in this case."

"I am afraid you are right," agreed Alan uncomfortably.

"My name, while respectable, is far from impressive, and the head of my family, Uncle Charles Rand, is a country squire with no pretensions to gentility. Besides, he and Aunt Henga have cast me off."

"By Jove, you are in the devil of a pucker, are you not?" sympathized Alan. "I wish I could help you, truly!"

While Todd was muttering irritably that they'd best put Missy in the coach and send her back to London, since he much doubted Master Alan's people would want to be flummoxed with that sort of row, Pommy recalled an earlier scheme.

"Do you have any idea how one becomes a servingmaid in an inn such as this?"

"It's a sure thing our host here wouldn't have you, after the brangle we put on outside in the yard," Alan said ruefully. "But wait! I think I have it! Isabelle Boggs is a good-hearted female, for all she's such a—that is," as he caught Pommy's minatory glance, "she's the one to help you find a place. Much better *ton* to have a female your sponsor, Pommy, I assure you."

"I believe you are right," said the girl after a minute's consideration. "Then I must ask you to arrange for the hire of a vehicle which will take me back to London at once."

"I shall do so as soon as we have finished eating," promised Alan.

"Now," corrected Pommy firmly, "for in that way no time will be lost. I must be back in Portman Square before the Ball begins. Lady Masterson will be greatly distressed, otherwise."

"She'll be sendin' out the Runners," said Todd glumly.

"It's nearly five, Pommy," said Alan remorsefully.

"That is not too late, if I get away smartly. Lady Masterson has bidden her guests for ten o'clock. It is the very height of elegance!"

"Damfoolery," muttered Todd, as he followed his two young charges out of the inn.

Nineteen

MINE HOST HAD BUSTLED to good effect, and within half an hour, well fed and in better spirits, Alan prepared to hand Pommy up into the hired chaise. He caught at her shoulder as she prepared to mount.

"Forgive me, Pommy! I truly meant it for the best! And forgive this wretched carriage, also! I can only hope you will not be smothered by the time you reach Portman Square!"

Pommy had turned to pat the hand upon her shoulder as a magnificent equipage swung to a dust-haloed stop behind them. From it decanted two very big men with faces like thunder. Glancing over Alan's shoulders, Pommy's mouth opened.

"Trouble, Alan!" she whispered. "On guard!"

Alan whirled to see the Earl and Colonel Rand bearing down upon him, their expressions clear warrant of their bloodthirsty intentions. It appeared to be a race to see which of the angry gentlemen could reach him first. Alan dropped his hand from Pommy's shoulder and faced his attackers with a rather sickly smile.

The big men had reached him, and towered over him in a bloodcurdling manner. Both men glanced quickly at Pommy.

"You are unhurt?" snapped the colonel.

"Are you safe, Pommy?" asked the Earl at the same time.

"I am very well," said Pommy hastily. *"Truly—"*

"My right, I think," said the colonel harshly, and turned upon the unfortunate Corcran.

"I claim the honor," insisted the Earl, jostling in ahead of his military companion. "I intend to teach this miserable little cur not to put his filthy paws on Pommy."

"I say," protested Alan feebly, and then, reading the icy determination in Lord Austell's eyes, shrugged and put up his fists as bravely as he could.

Pommy caught her wits together and thrust herself between the two. "If you are going to behave like a pair of gamecocks, perhaps you will have the kindness to permit Alan to see me off to London first, in the coach he has just hired for that purpose. Then you may all batter each other into insensibility for all I care! I am sure Lady Masterson will not miss either of you at her first Ball since her return to Society!"

Lord Austell paused and his eyes went quickly to the girl's pale, determined face. Slowly the icy glare faded, and he shook his head as though coming out of a frenzy. "I was afraid he had hurt you," he muttered.

"I *told* you he had not," retorted Pommy, crossly. "You never listen to what I say."

Colonel Rand, also less tense, said placatingly, "We have driven hell-for-leather from London in a panic lest your life or—uh—honor might have been endangered, Pommy. You must make allowances for the fears of those who love you."

The girl shot a quick glance at the Earl's set face. "Oh! then I am truly grateful, but you see that I should return at once if Lady Masterson's party is not to be spoiled for her."

The Earl had himself well in hand. "You will, of course, return in my carriage with your uncle and myself," he began formally.

"But Alan has already paid to rent this coach for me," began Pommy.

"*Shut up, Pommy,*" advised Alan desperately, "and just *go,* will you?"

For some obscure masculine reason, probably connected with the sudden releasing of the tension under which they had labored for several hours, both the colonel and the Earl burst into laughter at this very practical advice from one who had no desire to be a battered Hero, much less a battered Villain. The colonel was about to hand Pommy into the Earl's carriage when a smart curricle, going much too fast, whirled past them and then was expertly brought back to the front of the inn. Gareth descended, accompanied by a white-faced but grimly enduring Chelm. The corners of Lord Austell's mouth quirked upward, but he said nothing, merely glancing toward Pommy as if to share his amusement with her. More rescuers! he seemed to be saying. Pommy fought to control her own laughter.

As Gareth and Chelm approached the unfortunate Alan, the young peer was shouting, "Name your seconds, Corcran! I will meet you this instant!"

The young footman had regained his breath, and was heard to offer to mill the hellhound down, either before or after the duel, whichever was most convenient.

Alan spread his palms and lifted his shoulders in an

210

expression of defeat. "This does not appear to be my lucky day," he said wryly to Lord Austell. "Perhaps if I might explain," he offered to Gareth.

That young man stared around him with bewilderment at his now-smiling uncle and Pommy.

"I say—isn't everyone angry at Corcran?"

This was greeted with another shout of laughter, in which Alan and Gareth finally joined, rather sheepishly.

Chelm, however, was made of less forgiving stuff. While the gentry were laughing off the insult to Miss Pommy, he got himself into position and swung a heavy fist at the young reprobate. Since Alan was not alert for attack, the blow connected neatly and he went down.

Pommy shrieked with alarm, but the three men stood looking down at the fallen abductor with wide smiles.

"A neat, flush hit." The colonel commended Chelm. "Had you thought of enlisting, young man?"

"He did deserve something for his cow-handed behavior," decided Lord Austell.

Gareth merely stared from one to the other in complete bewilderment.

"Is no one going to do anything for poor Alan?" demanded Pommy glaring around the circle.

"Shouldn't think there'd be much to do," pronounced the Earl judicially. "He'll come round shortly."

A stocky old man thrust his way into the group. "Gave him a settler, did ye?" he inquired. "Well, I'll not deny he's been asking for it." He checkd over the limp body with some expertise. "A nice clean blow. He'll be around again in a minute," was Todd's opinion. "Just leave him to me, I've watched over him since he was a lad. Powerful self-willed, is Mr. Alan. Maybe this'll learn him some sense."

"Shall we be on our way back to London?" the Earl asked Pommy sweetly. "I believe you were most anxious to set out."

"I shall never understand men," said Pommy, with a final worried glance at the still supine youth. She allowed Colonel Rand to take her arm and lead her to the Earl's luxurious carriage. Lord Austell had a word with Gareth while Pommy's uncle handed the girl up into the vehicle and followed her into it. Then Lord Austell went around to the off-side and mounted. George Rand silently saluted this strategic tactical maneuver, which placed the Earl on Pommy's left and the colonel on her right, instead of leaving the colonel sitting bodkin between them. His grin was not obvious in the gloom of the closed carriage, and in any event neither Milord nor Pommy was much interested in anything but one another. Rather distraitly, Lord Austell gave his coachman the office to drive out, and the great carriage rolled smoothly onto the highroad and headed toward London.

When they had paused momentarily to light the side lamps, the colonel glanced across his niece's head at the Earl.

"I suppose we must let the whole matter drop?"

"If my beef-witted heir had had his way about the duel, we should all have found ourselves an *on dit*. It is to be hoped we shall brush through without scandal if Aurora has not concocted some skip-brained ploy. She and my younger brother were forever coming up with absurd games from whose frequently unfortunate results I had to rescue them."

This statement found no favor with either of his hearers. The colonel merely stiffened a little but Pommy cried out against the harshness of the Earl's judgment. "Lady Masterson has been kindness itself to me! I

212

cannot remember my mother very well, but she could not have been more loving than Her Ladyship!" Pommy had kept her head so far, but it had been a long day. To her own horror as well as that of her two escorts, she began to cry. The immediate reaction of both gentlemen was to put a comforting arm around the weeping Heroine. Unfortunately, the carriage, though luxurious, was not room-sized, and the two big masculine arms collided somewhere above Pommy's head with a distinct thud.

The contact startled a smothered oath from both men, and a flailing readjustment, as a result of which Pommy ended up in the Earl's close clasp, while Colonel Rand drew back into his own corner of the coach.

"There would seem to be some matters for discussion between us, Austell," said George Rand coldly.

The Earl tightened his grasp upon the girl, who, in sheer surprise at his action, had ceased to weep. "Our first business, Rand, is to get to Aurora's dam-*dashed* party," he snapped, in a very un-Romantic tone. "I must be there not only to scotch any rumors about this abduction, but more importantly to prevent my rather whimsical sister-in-law from embroiling us all in something which *will* provide fresh fodder for the gabble-mongers. Am I correct, sir, in thinking that *you* might have something to ask *me*? As head of Aurora's family, I mean?"

This was carrying the battle to the enemy's camp indeed. The gallant officer stiffened with shock, hemmed, hawed, and finally said to the younger man in almost a petulant tone, "I would have chosen a more suitable place for a discussion of such importance and confidentiality, Milord, but—"

"Yes, you may wed my sister-in-law with my blessing, Rand," interrupted Lord Austell matter-of-factly, "and I shall be greatly obliged to you. It is a relief to know there will be someone with a firm hand to keep her rather colorful notions under control."

Before the colonel could voice his objections to this offhand treatment of what was to him a Very Solemn Moment, Pommy had interrupted, eyes alight with interest.

"Uncle George, are you to wed my dear employer? But this is beyond anything famous! When was it contrived? I had no inkling of it!"

The colonel blessed the comparative gloom of the carriage, lit only by two small candles in glass lanterns, for hiding the color he could feel burning in his cheeks. "Why, Pommy, it . . . that is to say—"

"She got him to ask her today," said the Earl, unforgivably.

"Sir!" began the colonel furiously.

"I hope you are not planning to cry off?" challenged the Earl, eyes brightly wicked with amusement. "That was a very convincing maneuver you executed just before we left Portman Square."

"It will be the best thing in the world for her!" cried Pommy with enthusiasm. "She has *so* needed a strong right arm!"

"And—er—other things." The Earl was apparently enjoying the situation all too well. "Very therapeutic."

"Milord," Colonel Rand began ominously, "your levity leads you beyond what is acceptable."

"Surely not unacceptable—within the marriage bond?" teased Milord.

But he had underestimated his opponent. In a voice they had not heard before, Colonel Rand inquired, silkily, "Have you forgotten that *I* am the head of Melpomene's family, Austell? I should not wish to have to make different arrangements for her."

There was a shocked silence, and then:

"A hit! A very palpable hit!" quoted Derek in a much subdued tone. "You must forgive me if I have transgressed the bounds of propriety in my speech, Rand. My excuse must be that I am little drunk with relief at having Pommy safe and secure with—with us." In an excess of decorum he removed his arm from around the girl and sat back into his corner of the carriage. Pommy was too worried by the apparent coolness between the two men to offer any conversational gambits, and the rest of the ride, mercifully fairly short, was taken in silence. Pommy was first to be dropped off, the carriage then went round to the colonel's lodging, and finally deposited the Earl at his own Town house with barely time to dress for Lady Masterson's Ball.

Twenty

AT TEN O'CLOCK precisely the spacious entrance
hall at Number Three Portman Square began to re-
sound to the thunder of the brass knocker. Mikkle
waved a hand imperiously, and a white-bewigged footman hurried forward to open the door for the first
arrivals. Lady Masterson, superb in violet satin and
diamonds, waited to welcome her guests at the top of
the great staircase. Standing beside her, Gareth was
breathtakingly handsome in dark purple velvet with a
mauve and silver waistcoat. Lord Austell, waiting
nearby to lead the guests to the ballroom, wondered
idly if they had planned their costumes to complement
one another so effectively. But there was no time for
idle musing, for Mikkle was directing a growing stream
of guests to the stairway to be received by Lady
Masterson. In the next half hour the door was never
closed, and the guests gradually filled the ballroom.

Lady Masterson was radiant. Her gallant hussar had arrived promptly, looking larger than life in his splendid dress uniform. As he bent over her white hand, he murmured a special greeting which brought a rosy glow to Her Ladyship's cheeks. Gareth, on the other hand, seemed ill at ease, turning his glance constantly toward the front door, and when, by ten-thirty, Miss Isabelle Boggs had not yet put in an appearance, he sought out his uncle who was acting as host in the ballroom until Lady Masterson left her post.

"Miss Boggs has not yet come," Gareth said anxiously. "Can something have happened to her? Can her father have prevented her—?"

"My poor boy." The Earl commiserated with him. "If you intend to wed your Isabelle, you will be compelled to learn patience. It is my understanding that the lady is congenitally incapable of arriving anywhere on time. Shall you find that too annoying?"

"Not if I can be assured that she is safe," averred the love-smitten youth stoutly. Then his face brightened. "We shall most likely spend the greater part of our time at Tory Hall, and I shall be able to supervise her activities. I am confident I can soon teach her to be punctual!"

"My *poor* boy!" the Earl reiterated, moved by the sight of such cocksure innocence. However, being a kindly man as well as a very worldly one, he made no attempt to disillusion the deluded youth.

At this moment the orchestra struck up a stately tune, and the Earl prepared to lead his sister-in-law into the first figure. Gareth returned to the head of the stairway, ostensibly to welcome late-arriving guests, although Mikkle was quite capable of ushering any such to the ballroom. His devotion was awarded; the door opened one more time to reveal the beautiful Miss

217

Boggs, awesomely lovely in white and gold, and accompanied correctly by her abigail. Gareth ran lightly down the stairs to welcome her.

He took her hand in his, and each stared into the other's face with a sort of innocent satisfaction.

"Does your father know you are here?" asked Gareth presently, beginning to lead his love up the staircase to the ballroom.

"Oh, yes," said Isabelle. "I had to tell him where I was going, at this hour in this dress. It is new. Do you like it?"

"It is the most beautiful dress I have ever seen," Gareth said simply. "Or perhaps you are the most beautiful girl I have ever seen." He stopped on the stairs and scrutinized girl and dress carefully. "It is very pretty," he decided, "but then I am sure I should think anything *you* wore was pretty." He led her upward again. "You say your father found out you were coming here? He was not angry?"

"Far from it," said Isabelle. "I should rather say, highly pleased. He thinks I am here to meet the Earl of Austell."

Gareth halted her again, this time on the wide landing outside the ballroom. The first dance was coming to an end. Gareth said quickly, "You are to save all your dances for me, remember! And my uncle had better announce our engagement at supper—that is, after he announces my mother's. Will that be agreeable to you, my dear Isabelle?"

"Your mother's—? I am sure it will be agreeable to me, if you and she are happy about it. Whom is she to marry?"

"Pommy's uncle, I believe, from what she says—although I was so late getting back here after rescuing Pommy that I got the merest outline. No, really, Isabelle," when she evidenced a tendency to be curious about his afternoon's adventure, "you have not answered *my* question, and it is more important than anything which occurred in Surrey—a very dull business indeed, for Pommy was apparently in no danger, and Chelm knocked Corcran down before I had a chance to call him out. No," he resisted further inquiry on her part, "you must answer *my* question before everyone comes prying and gabbling and trying to get you away from me. What is your answer, Isabelle?"

"I forgot the question," Miss Boggs confessed, with an enchantingly pretty smile.

Gareth beamed at her. "You are teasing me, little rogue! Or do you just wish for me to ask you again?"

"Yes," said Miss Boggs, sensibly choosing the path of least resistance.

"Is Uncle Derek to announce *our* engagement during supper? *Do* say he may, Isabelle!"

"I should like that very well. Then Papa cannot force Lord Austell to marry me."

"No one shall force you to marry anyone but me," promised Gareth. "Ah! the dance is ended! Let us find my uncle and tell him what we have decided."

While the two innocents were moving through the crowded room seeking Lord Austell, that nobleman was considering launching a search of his own. All the time he had been dancing with Lady Masterson, he had looked in vain for one slight, girlish figure. As the dance ended, he said to his sister-in-law in a voice charged with exasperation, "My dear Aurora, one can hardly see one's hand before one's face in this Arcadian gloom! Whose bird-brained idea was it to turn the ballroom into a bosky dell?"

"Mine," said Her Ladyship crisply. "You'd like it too, if you had Melpomene on your arm instead of me."

Recalled to his duty, the Earl grinned ruefully and said all that was proper to his hostess, and then, with a coaxing smile, added, *"Dear* Aurora, where is my Pommy?"

"In her room," answered Lady Masterson.

The Earl's smile vanished. "Why have you kept her there?"

"I?" said Her Ladyship. "Both Gordon and I tried without avail to get the chit down here! She refuses to come!"

"Have you any idea why?"

"I think she is afraid I am going to embarrass you by announcing your engagement."

"To whom?" thundered the Earl.

"For Heaven's sake, Austell, moderate your voice!" commanded Her Ladyship. "You are attracting attention!"

"To whom?" gritted the Earl, *sotto voce*.

"Why, to Melpomene, of course," replied Her Ladyship with a naughty smile. "It has given her such exquisite agony to plan to refuse you for your own good! She should be allowed one chance to be the Blighted Heroine!"

The Earl glared down at her. "Aurora, if you have put her off me with your tricks—!"

"If the chit is so easily put off, she could hardly have been said to be *on,* Derek," advised his old friend. "Her room is the second door down the corridor after my sitting room." Lady Masterson smiled and bowed to two middle-aged gallants who were bearing down on her purposefully. Behind them, to the rescue, loomed the colorful figure of Colonel Rand. "Get back here before supper," she called softly after His Lordship's departing figure. "You have two announcements to make!"

The Earl sent a piratical glance over his shoulder as he made ruthlessly for the door through the press. "Three!" he said.

When the Earl came to the door of Aurora's sitting room, he counted two more doors carefully. Standing in the luxurious, well-lighted hallway, he made a Romantic figure indeed in his black velvet and white satin. He was a big, well-built man, with a handsome imperturbable face, and he well knew his world and his own position in it, yet he suddenly felt himself trembling with all the ardor and uncertainty of a callow youth. He raised his hand to knock, then hesitated. Sounds of music came faintly from the ballroom below. Squaring his shoulders, he rapped sharply.

"Who—who is it?" came Pommy's voice from within.

"Whom would you wish it to be?" asked the Earl, pretending to insouciance he did not feel.

"Milord!" There was a sound of rapid footsteps, and the door was flung wide. Framed in the opening was a slender figure in softly shimmering white and silver. Upon her sweetly rounded breast, and moving with her breath, the Earl's emerald matched the green fire in Pommy's eyes.

"It is you! I was afraid—! That is—is anything wrong?"

The Earl was forced to take himself sternly in hand. He was finding the lovely little figure as dazzling as though he had been no more than the veriest youth.

"Yes, there is a great deal wrong," he replied, unable to take his eyes from the piquant little face under the pile of night-black hair. "Are you going to ask me in, or must I announce the sad story to anyone passing in the hall?"

"Oh, come in, Milord!" urged Pommy, her face quick with alarm. "What has happened?"

Inside, with the door safely closed behind him, the Earl began to enjoy his game. "I am in deepest despair," he announced quietly.

Pommy's beautiful eyes opened even wider. "What is it, dear sir? Can you tell me?"

"I am about to be publicly humiliated," intoned the Earl.

Pommy wrung her hands, her eyes on his. "How?"

"There is to be an announcement at supper—"

Pommy groaned. "Oh, yes! I *knew* it would be so! Can you not exercise enough control over Lady Masterson to prevent it?"

"I am to announce Lady Masterson's engagement to—"

"Lady Masterson? But I thought she—my uncle—that is—"

"Yes, Her Ladyship is to marry your uncle," said the Earl, with what he hoped was a heartbroken sigh.

"Does—does it distress you very greatly?" asked the girl, white faced.

Observing her anxious expression, the Earl took shame to himself and began to smile. "No, I'm delighted to get her off my hands," he admitted coolly. "And I think Rand's the very man who can manage her, and prevent any more of these naughty ploys of hers."

Pommy looked puzzled. "But if you do not mind?" she began.

"That is not the whole of it," said the Earl relentlessly. "I have also to announce Gareth's engagement—"

"Oh, not to me, surely? He is so happy with his Isabelle!"

"To his Isabelle," concluded Lord Austell. "And you do see where that leaves me, do you not?"

222

Pommy stared up into his dark, smiling face, her heart in her eyes. "No . . . that is, I do not quite see the problem as yet—"

"I shall be publicly humiliated! The only member of my immediate family not yet spoken for! Left to wither on the vine, unwanted, unregarded—! With the cream of Society present to witness my plight!"

Gradually the expression on Pommy's face changed. The Earl caught his breath, of a sudden most fearful that his dramatic scene had miscued. He watched her eyelids fall over the lustrous eyes. Long lashes shadowed her cheeks. She seemed in a daze.

"Pommy—my dearest girl—are you feeling all right?"

Waving this belated concern away with one hand, Pommy once again looked into his face. "And how had you hoped I might help you in this—imbroglio?"

The Earl took her hand in his. "I had hoped very much indeed that you might consent to allow me to make three announcements instead of two," he said quietly, all laughter gone from his face.

"You consider me a suitable match?" asked the girl, directly.

"I am desperately hoping that *you* will consider a man who is no longer young, who lacks the fresh enthusiasm you deserve—"

"That is silly," said Pommy forthrightly. "You must know you are wonderful."

The Earl caught a joyful breath. "Would you care to enlarge upon that?"

His gaze was held by Pommy's lovely eyes as closely as if he were mesmerized.

"You are more beautiful than Gareth and braver than the Colonel and much more fun to be with than Alan Corcran," said Pommy succinctly. "In fact, you are the most wonderful man in the world."

"I shall settle for that," said the Earl, humbly, "as long as you continue to believe it. Oh, my dearest Pommy, please say you will marry me!"

"I love you," Pommy continued clearly. "If you do not love me, I shall be unhappy as long as I live."

The Earl's head came up quickly from where he had bent it to kiss her hand. "Pommy, you are not going to decide to be Blighted and ruin my life, are you?"

"No," said Pommy gently. "I have found that it is too painful to be Blighted when it is really so, and not a Romantic game."

The Earl's shoulders sagged with relief. "I have discovered that I am an even greater Romantic than you. For me, no ending will do but the classic one."

"What?" asked Pommy, still dazed by the wonder of this whole conversation.

"Of course you know it! We must Live Happily Ever After," the Earl instructed her, and took his Pommy into his arms.